D1443510

Bread
on
Arrival

Also by Lou Jane Temple

A Stiff Risotto
Revenge of the Barbeque Queens
Death by Rhubarb

Bread
on
Arrival

LOU JANE TEMPLE

ST. MARTIN'S PRESS ≈ NEW YORK

Library of Congress Cataloging-in-Publication Data

Temple, Lou Jane.
    Bread on arrival / Lou Jane Temple. — 1st ed.
      p.   cm.
    Includes index.
    ISBN 0-312-19244-4
    I.   Title.
    PS3570.E535B74   1998
    813'.54—dc21   98-22316
                                          CIP

First Edition: November 1998

10 9 8 7 6 5 4 3 2 1

To my children,
Phillip, Jed and Reagan
with all my love

Acknowledgments

The more books I write, the more I realize how many people help me along the way.

Playwright Ron Megee read the early rough version and gave creative counsel. Margaret Silva and Rozanne Gold gave much needed support, psychic and otherwise. Dean Dixon surfed the net to research biogenetics. My friends at Farm to Market Bread answered lots of silly bread questions. Judith Fertig provided valuable wheat history.

Thanks to David Gibson for taking me on a tour of his grain elevator. Thanks also to the the Kansas City Board of Trade, the American Institute of Baking and Milling, and Baking News for lots of information. Sharon and Gil Nanez loaned me their island retreat to write.

Blessings on all your houses, my friends.

If you are interested in the art of bread baking, here are some books that helped me enormously.

Bread Alone, Daniel Leader and Judith Blahnik, William Morrow.

Brother Juniper's Bread Book, Peter Reinhart, Addison-Wesley Publishing.

English Bread and Yeast Cookery, Elizabeth David, Biscuit Books.

The Italian Baker, Carol Field, Harper & Row.

Secrets of Jesuit Breadmaking, Brother Rick Curry, Harper Perennial Press.

Prologue

The young man slipped out of the water quietly. He was naked. This little river ran through his family's farm and he had been swimming in it his whole life. It had never been as amazing as it was tonight, as glorious, as revealing. Everywhere he looked there were shimmering silver disks: they glittered on his body, in the water, on the ground and trees. Inside every silver disk was an entire universe. Tiny spheres orbited around exploding brilliant suns, deep black holes of magnetism so strong he was sucked into every one of them, belts of floating asteroids flickering as they darted along.

The young man laughed. He now knew the secrets of the universe. All those years of Sunday school, of church services. How foolish they seemed. He wished for a moment that his parents were here, his sisters. He would explain to them how everything worked.

Suddenly the ground moved. An ugly crack in the earth appeared right by the young man's feet. It threatened to swallow him, wanted to swallow him. He cried out for help, rolling as far away from the crack as he could on the flat Kansas ground. This ground that he had worked since he was a child, that had given him calloused hands and strong, muscled arms had turned against him with a vengeance. He was crawling now on his hands and knees, whimpering like a baby, trying to escape the underground that seemed determined to catch him, suck him into its bosom. Then the young man had a brilliant idea. He would climb a tree.

He ran back to the river's edge where the cottonwood leaves rustled. He shimmied up the broad trunk of an old cottonwood, scraping his thighs. Blood appeared on his legs, his clawing fingers, the blood also glittering with the same silver disks he saw everywhere around him. He arrived at the V in the trunk, where two thick arms of the tree went in opposite directions to the stars. There he rested, shivering, cold, bleeding, but triumphant. The earth hadn't swallowed him like it had intended.

In an hour or so, the voices became too loud for him to rest any longer. They were calling him. He must find them. He jumped to the ground, a good twelve or fifteen feet below. His ankle twisted and snapped with the impact but the young man didn't care. He looked around for the voices. The voices were coming from down the train tracks. Down the tracks where the sun was coming up. No, there were two suns, next to each other, coming toward him. And the voices, so loud, calling him. He would go to meet them. Go to the twin suns. What an amazing universe, the young man thought as he ran, dragging his bad leg down the train tracks in the night.

Sweet Pepper Bread

1 sweet red pepper
1 sweet yellow pepper
2 T. olive oil
2 tsp. dry yeast
1 ¼ cups warm water
4 cups bread flour
2 tsp. salt

Roast the peppers by placing them in a shallow baking dish, drizzling them with olive oil and kosher salt, covering them with foil. Bake for 40–50 minutes at 350 degrees, until the peppers are soft. Cool, pull the skins off and finely chop the peppers.

Stir the yeast into the water. Let stand until creamy, about 10 minutes. Add the oil and peppers, then the flour and salt. Knead 5 minutes. Place the dough in an oiled bowl, cover with a clean towel or plastic wrap, let rise until doubled, about 1 hour.

Punch down the dough and knead a minute. Divide the dough in two and shape into round loaves. Put on baking sheet sprinkled with cornmeal, let rise again for 1 hour.

Heat the oven to 450 degrees. Place the loaves in the

oven and spray the sides of the inner oven with water using a plastic spray bottle. Immediately reduce the heat to 400 degrees. Bake 35 minutes, spraying twice with water. Cool completely before cutting into bread.

One

Heaven Lee was pouting. "They said my gluten network was uneven."

Pauline Kramer, the baker at Cafe Heaven, looked at her boss sympathetically. Pauline had finished her bread baking for the day many hours before and was now icing a burnt sugar cake with caramel-flavored icing. "That's why we use the Hobart to knead bread in this day and age instead of brute strength. But you have to learn to do it by hand first, the old-fashioned way. Making bread is very mysterious and very scientific at the same time. Chemistry and all that." She ended her speech with a smug little smile toward Heaven.

"I know, I know," Heaven replied crossly. "I guess the perfectionist hiding deep inside me had its ego wounded. No one has ever told me my gluten was unacceptable before."

Pauline smiled that smile again. It was great having the superior position for a change. "You're doing fine," she said grandly. "You didn't even understand what gluten was six months ago. Maybe one of your arms is stronger than the other and your kneading is uneven," Pauline offered. "One of mine is. I had uneven gluten too, until I learned to favor my left arm while kneading."

Heaven had been cradling her loaf of bread in her arms like a new-born baby, wrapped loosely as it was in a kitchen towel. She placed it reverently on one of the work tables. Pauline came over and pulled off a chunk, bit into it, and chewed. Heaven looked at her expectantly.

"Well, your crust is nice, it's a good thickness and it's crisp. But you can see what they were talking about with the crumb, can't you?" Pauline's finger was pointing to the center of the loaf. There was a streak of dough that looked like it had been cut with a dull knife, all gummy and stuck together. "And you probably didn't help matters when you formed your loaf. A lot can go wrong when you're forming your loaves," Pauline said with the confidence of someone who had mastered loaf forming herself.

Brian Hoffman, the lunch chef and day prep cook had been taking in this conversation from his station on the other side of the table. He couldn't stand it another minute. "What are you two talking about? What's the crumb? I don't see any crumbs."

Pauline gave him a withering look. "For your information, the crumb refers to the texture of the interior of a loaf of bread. We judge the crumb by whether it is even or uneven. Does it have big holes? Is it dry or is it gummy? Stuff like that," Pauline said with the authority of a Culinary Institute instructor.

Brian shrugged, unimpressed. Even if he were interested in the baker's art he sure wouldn't let Pauline know it now. "Who knew," he said nonchalantly. "I thought you just threw together some yeast and flour and water," knowing that was sure to get Pauline where she lived.

Heaven smiled and pinched off a piece of her crust, popping it in her mouth. She looked more confident and nodded to Pauline, as if to confirm Pauline's approval of the crispiness. "Brian, gluten is what makes raised bread. The wheat proteins interact to form this loopy chain of molecules, kinda like a slinky. Thanks to the gluten, the wheat dough expands to incorporate the carbon dioxide produced by the yeast. That's what makes bread rise. Cool, huh? I must confess, Brian, I was almost as stupid about bread as you are. No offense, honey."

Brian grinned as he sliced eggplant. "None taken. I'm a cook, not a baker." He looked up slyly and added, "A lover, not a fighter."

Heaven hurried on, not wanting a war to begin between Pauline and Brian over which was more important to humanity in general, cooking or baking. "Pauline is one of the board members of this national bread bakers group, ARTOS, which is Greek or something for bread." Pauline looked up proudly, and Heaven continued. "So I joined and I'm taking a beginning bread workshop. It certainly has taken me down a peg or two. I thought I knew everything I needed to about the kitchen, but this bread making is really an art. I also feel terrible about the conditions Pauline has to work in."

With that Pauline adopted a martyred expression. Brian wasn't buying it. He looked around the small kitchen. It was cramped but Heaven had bought every gadget and piece of equipment they had ever requested. It didn't look that bad to him. "Pauline, what have you been whining to the boss about now?"

Pauline's jaw tightened, but before she could answer Brian, Heaven jumped in again. "Brian, it's a miracle that we have the quality of bread we do. Most of the bakers in the Kansas City chapter of ARTOS have big deck ovens, or wood burning European ovens. Pauline just makes do with the ovens in the stoves and the convection oven and lots of improvisation, like spritzing the loaves with a spray bottle of water and pans of water in the oven and pizza stones to bake on."

Brian grinned, ready to make peace. "Yeah, ol' Olive Oyl is a champ. You can't beat that sweet red pepper bread she concocted. Especially when you slather that goat cheese spread of yours, Heaven, on top of it."

Pauline, who did resemble Popeye's animated girlfriend in appearance, smiled but there was still malice in her eyes. Heaven saw more spats in the offing, and she wasn't willing to referee forever. "Are you two OK with the dinner prep?" she asked. "If you are, I'm going to check out Mona and Sal, see what's been happening on 39th Street today."

"We're cool, H." Brian said with his head down, concentrating. Pauline was lost in her cakes, icing carefully as she spun the stainless steel wheel the cake was sitting on.

Heaven passed through the empty dining room, poured herself a cup of coffee, and went out the front door. It was the middle of the afternoon, a lazy time in the restaurant, after lunch and before the night crew arrived.

On 39th Street, next to Cafe Heaven, was The Cat's Meow, a store full of cat stuff; earrings and posters and rhinestone cat collars. Mona Kirk was the store's owner and one of Heaven's good friends. Heaven knocked on the window and caught Mona's attention as she was writing up the ticket for a little blue-haired lady who was buying a bejeweled cat food dish. Heaven jerked her head across the street towards Sal's Barber Shop and Mona nodded. Heaven didn't wait but cut across the block toward Sal's.

39th Street was the heart of midtown Kansas City, Missouri. Neither chic nor slum, the crosstown street had a little of both in the mix of businesses and people who lived and worked there. A business street right in the heart of a residential neighborhood, instead of in a strip mall or designated shopping area, was unusual for Kansas City. In New York this was par for the course; business and residential had always coexisted. In Kansas City, the business owners and home owners struggled to get along.

The businesses that brought lots of cars, like Cafe Heaven, had upset the neighbors who didn't like strangers parking in front of their houses, making it hard for them and their families to find parking. Heaven and the others had rented a parking lot just down the street from the cafe and across from another busy bar, helping the relationship between business and home owners considerably.

On their part, Heaven and the other business owners wished some of the home owners would spruce up their yards and paint their houses. Many of the homes had been passed down to sons and daughters no longer living in Kansas City. They had become rental houses that didn't get the love and attention they needed. Recently a new group of young couples were buying property around 39th Street, and gradually lawns were resown with bluegrass seed, roofs were repaired, paint was applied.

In the long run, Heaven liked that the neighbors and the businesses weren't all gentrified. A new store selling fifties collectibles was next to an old dry cleaners that was next to a bar frequented by the interns and nurses from the medical center a few blocks away. New restaurants popped up often now, but the tattoo parlor stayed open and busy as well. The linchpin of this neighborhood, just east of the dividing line between Kansas and Missouri, was Sal's barber shop. Sal cut the hair of business moguls and waiters, students and professors. When the famous filmmakers Merchant and Ivory made *Mr. and Mrs. Bridge* in Kansas City, Sal cut Paul Newman's hair to give it the right vintage flair.

Sal also knew everything that was going on in Kansas City. He could get information out of a CIA agent or a priest if necessary. A mere mortal spilled his guts gratefully to Sal.

"Heaven, where have you been today?" he asked while running the clippers around the sideburn of a young, male art-student type.

Heaven plopped down on one of the many Naugehyde and chrome chairs lining the shop's walls. She checked out her own bright red locks in the mirror. Sal had cut it short again for her just last week. It was punk spiked but trying to curl. She attempted to straighten it out with her hands, pushing it up into place. "At a bread making class. My gluten was uneven, and I got called down for it."

Sal smiled without dislodging the unlit cigar in his mouth. "You can get into trouble anywhere, can't you? Did Pauline quit?"

Heaven shook her head. "Of course not," she said haughtily, as if no one ever quit their job in her restaurant. "There's a new movement across America to bake real bread again, and Pauline and I are members of a new bread club and they're having their annual conference here, starting at the end of the week, what with this being the breadbasket of America and all and . . ."

"Stop, whoa, I'm missing something. Wait to say another word till I get situated." It was Mona Kirk, who had put a "back in ten minutes" sign on her door and crossed the street for a coffee klatch. She poured a cup of Sal's inky brew. It poured more like molasses than coffee. Mona sat down next to Heaven, eager for news. "Who's coming to town?"

Heaven slipped her arm through her friend's and gave a squeeze. "Cute earrings." Mona had a mouse earring on one ear and a cat earring on the other. "Well, all over the country, bread bakers are making bread with wild yeasts and baking in old-fashioned ovens fired by coal and wood and they have this group . . ."

Mona interrupted again. "Old-fashioned and expensive as gold. Why, I went to that La Brea Bakery in L.A. when I was at the gift show last year. They have this chocolate cherry bread that costs eight dollars a loaf. It was good though."

Sal turned his head on that news. Sal was a master at keeping up with events and conversation through the mirrors lining the walls of the shop. It really took something to get him to actually turn toward a speaker. "Eight bucks for a loaf of bread? Why, that's how much I charge for a haircut. Is that what they're teaching you, Heaven? How to make eight-buck bread?"

"No, Sal, I know that would never fly in the home of white bread," Heaven answered defensively. "I just want to know how to make a good loaf of sourdough. Our chapter is hosting this conference, and we're having one of the dinners at the cafe. And of course I *am* from Kansas, where most of the wheat in the world comes from," Heaven boasted, knowing she was exaggerating. "There's a field trip to Manhattan, Kansas, one day to some research place. Famous bakers are coming from all over the world, including Germany and Italy."

Mona couldn't resist. "I guess that means lots of dough for Kansas City," she cracked with a straight face.

Sal and Heaven both moaned. "Yeah," Sal said as he undid the smock protecting the art student's leather jacket from hair fallout. "A bread convention is about right for this town. New Orleans gets the racy stuff, the lawyers and pipe fitters who want a wild time. We get the bread bakers."

Heaven stood up and tried to simulate a huff. "Who cares about dumb old lawyers," she asked, knowing Sal would probably remind her she used to be one. "Bread bakers are good. Kansas City is in the middle of wheat country so we should like bread bakers. And they, the ARTOS folks, need to visit the futures market and experimental farms and see new wheat clones and stuff. They need to know the roots of their art or industry, whichever you call it." Heaven wasn't done yet. "And you know, Sal, the largest white bread bakery in the country, probably the world, is right here in Kansas City, BIG BREAD," she said just the way the Chamber of Commerce would have wanted. Then she realized she'd better qualify that boasting. "Not that any of us artisans care about that kind of bread." Sal rolled his eyes. Eight-dollar bread indeed.

Mona stood up, too. There was a customer peering in the window of the cat shop. "Heaven, don't let Sal get you going. I'm sure the bread convention will be very nice. I've got a live one across the street. See you later," she said as she put down her coffee and walked out the door.

"I'm right behind you," Heaven said. "After all, it's Monday and the open mike is tonight. We'll be busy, like every Monday night."

"Don't go away mad, H," Sal called over his shoulder with a chuckle. Heaven had been an easy mark today. She riled up fast.

Heaven stuck her head back in the shop. "If you don't

watch out I'll make you eat the bread I baked," she said and then stuck her tongue out at Sal and ducked out before he could get a retort in. As she crossed the street, she realized she was looking forward to the bread convention. It didn't even sound boring. Maybe she was getting old.

Goat Cheese Spread

10–12 cloves roasted garlic
Extra virgin olive oil
8–12 oz. goat cheese

Because there are only three ingredients in this spread, each one needs to be the best you can find. I'm partial to very olivey olive oil for this dish. The goat cheese can be French, or if you live in an area of the country where local goat cheese is produced, I'm sure your local product would be the thing to use. The garlic should be fresh and have no ammonia odor.

I like to have roasted garlic around all the time, so I would peel at least six heads of garlic and place the cloves in a shallow baking pan. Drizzle with good olive oil and kosher salt. The salt helps draw out the natural sugar in the garlic and produces the wonderful caramel color we are looking for. Cover the pan with foil and bake in a slow to medium oven about 40 minutes at 325–350 degrees. Uncover at this point. Your garlic should be soft and starting to turn brown. Bake uncovered for ten minutes. Cool and store in refrigerator. If you don't have the time or patience to peel garlic and already peeled cloves are not available to you, split whole heads of garlic in two and roast as we would the peeled cloves, with olive oil and kosher salt, with the cut side down. You have to squeeze the garlic out of the roasted heads like you would toothpaste, so you can't measure with great accuracy but I think a whole head's worth of garlic paste should be added to this amount of spread.

Place the goat cheese and the garlic in a food processor and turn on, drizzling in the olive oil while the processor is running until you reach a good spreading consistency. Use within 24 hours.

A great option is to change the kind of oil, from olive to walnut or hazelnut. This gives a wonderful change in the flavor of the spread.

Two

Sunlight hit the row of 'Illinois Bundle Flower' Walter Jinks was walking down, shading his eyes with an upheld hand as he walked. This first walk of the day was his favorite. It was just before seven and Walter had completed his rounds, an inspection tour that he made every morning. Central Kansas was still hot in September, and Walter wiped his brow with a faded red bandana.

These grasses and grains, the product of twenty-five years of work, were doing well. They had produced a crop of seeds this year that was a much better yield than last year. And now the plants were still working, their roots storing up nutrients, preparing for the cold weather. Next spring Walter was sure that these plants would produce again.

He stopped at the limestone building that had been a mill since farmers first came to this place, a hundred plus years ago. The wooden sluices for the water had been replaced, of course, and the grinding stones were now turned by a turbine engine most of the time instead of water power. Aside from those technical changes, the building had remained true to its purpose. Walter liked that. He stepped inside.

It was here that the graduate students who worked with him ground the various grains and grasses into flour, searching for the combination that would satisfy a world that loved wheat bread. As he idly opened the lids of the bins filled with ground vegetation, he straightened with pride. Nothing he had done before had the possibilities of this.

He had believed he was right when he led the Moratorium in Washington those many long years ago. He knew his efforts had helped LBJ decide not to run for the presidency again, perhaps had shortened that awful war. But that was just child's play.

If the world was going to accept bread made out of these flours, he knew he would have to improve the taste and texture; there was much left to do, but if the world could accept his work, the world could avert disaster. The annual monocultures, like wheat, that stripped the planet's topsoil would be history. His perennial grains would feed billions and not have to be replanted again and again. He thrust his hand into one of the bins and let the light brown meal flow between his fingers.

This conference of bread bakers next week was important. If the famous bakers would support his work, if they would bake bread with his flours, then the rest of the world would follow, he was sure of it. Even the guys from BIG BREAD. They had never paid any attention until now, never given him a cent for research. Now they would have to listen, if only for an hour or so.

There were some loaves of bread resting on the top of the work space, dusty with flour. Walter took a loaf with him to toast for breakfast. He stepped out of the mill and walked toward the farmhouse with the modern experimental kitchen built onto its modest frame. He looked across the road at his neighbor busy on his John Deere tractor, tillers cutting deep plows in the earth. A gust of wind took part of that Kansas field up in the air. It became a cloud of soil flying toward Oklahoma.

"What a waste," Walter muttered, shaking his head.

General Irwin Mills, U.S. Army retired, straightened his tie in the mirror. He wore a crisp white shirt, heavy starch, and a stolid navy blue tie with a small pattern that resembled a wheat sheaf. It had been a Christmas gift from his staff last year. Even on days like today, when he would spend most of his time in the test kitchens, he dressed in formal business attire, suit and tie. The general could go on at length about how dress code affects performance. Needless to say, there were no "casual Fridays" at the Milling and Grain International Studies Laboratory in Manhattan, Kansas. The general ran a boar-bristle brush quickly through his military-length gray hair. Every follicle was now standing at attention. He gave himself a full military salute in the mirror. "Carry on," he snapped at his own image, then wheeled and left the bathroom. No one had ever said that the general didn't set the same high standards for his own performance that he demanded of others. Even morning ablutions were performed by the book.

Before the general had taken over the research lab, an agronomist with a wife and family had run the place, living in a house on the other side of town. The general, however, had no family. His wife had died of cancer seven years before, two years before the general retired. They never had children. "Running around the world is no place for a child," the general pronounced early in his marriage, and his wife had placidly agreed, already unable to argue with her husband. So now the general lived alone and had requested an apartment outfitted above the office wing of the laboratory. He could be at work in forty-eight seconds, give or take three seconds. This morning he got there in forty-seven.

"How are you this morning, sir?" the chief test baker asked as the general marched into the spotless test kitchen. Although the baker had been working with the general almost twenty years, when General Mills was responsible for feeding every G.I. in the army, he had never called the general by his first name. He had never even considered it.

The general slipped off his suit jacket just as he had slipped it on a few minutes ago. He replaced it with a white lab coat, a white baker's cap, and then started putting on thin latex gloves. He resembled a surgeon getting ready for a morning of operations.

"Eager to get started," he said. "We have a bunch of idiot artisan bakers coming out here on Thursday. But the research and development team from BIG BREAD will be with them and some European bakers, even the largest millers in Rome. We must put on the dog-and-pony show." The general sounded irritated but resigned to the fact that occasionally outsiders would have to be tolerated. "We will be introducing our new genetically altered wheat clone. I want them to fall all over themselves to be the first to use this product." The general eyed the loaves of bread lined up with precision on the work table. "What are these?"

"I don't know, sir. They were here when I arrived this morning. They must be from research and development number three."

"Well, we better give them a try. The crust wasn't hard

enough yesterday. I know these artisans love crust on their bread. We've got to provide all the silly razzle-dazzle they're used to," the general said as he sliced a slice from each of the loaves, slices of exactly the same thickness.

The general's assistant gave him a mini salute. "They won't even know what hit 'em."

Ernest Powell smiled as he went down the stairs. He took a big gulp of air. There it was. There was nothing better than the smell of fresh baked bread. This morning it reminded him of his grandmother, as it always did. Of course his mother made good bread, too. They were all, all three generations, Kansas wheat farmers with bread in their blood. But his dear departed grandmother's bread was the best. Not even his own sweet Betsy's bread could compare.

Ernest saw three loaves of bread sitting on the kitchen counter. He wondered if Betsy had made those to take to the funeral yesterday. Ernest had to admit to himself it had been quite a while since he had tasted his wife's bread, now that he was the family bread baker most of the time. But they certainly weren't going to have day-old bread this morning.

He went over to the machine sitting on the kitchen counter and removed the pail resting within. A new burst of fragrance hit his nose. Ernest tapped the bottom of the pail and a loaf of bread fell on the counter, golden and still warm. Just then the back door of the house opened and his wife stepped into the kitchen, so pretty in her print dress with her hair pinned neatly in a net, as was the style of all Mennonite women. She was carrying a basket full of eggs that Ernest guessed she had just gathered from the hen house.

"What kind did you make for us this morning, Ernest my love," she asked as she, too, took a deep breath.

"Wheat berry," Ernest said with pride. "There are cooked wheat berries in the bread."

His wife started cracking eggs in a glass mixing bowl. "Your grandmother would have words for us both. You for enjoying such women's work as baking bread. Me for shirking one of my household duties."

Ernest put his arms around his wife and gave her a kiss on the top of her head as she worked. "All the great bakers of France are men, although that wouldn't stop Granny from disapproving. And we'd get an even longer lecture for making our bread in a bread machine," he laughed.

"Not if she knew you won the national championship," Betsy said with a laugh. "Now go wake the children, Mr. Grand Champion Bread Baker, I'm going to make baked eggs with lemon juice and powdered sugar this morning."

Ernest sat down at the kitchen table. "I'll get them in a minute. First I want to run through the speech that I'm giving at the ARTOS meeting for you. The kids will tease me."

"So will those fancy bread makers. They don't want people using that gadget that you're so proud of."

Ernest stood up, a warrior defending his turf. "Why? Because it fills the house with the blessed smell of homemade bread? It's a lot better than BIG BREAD, puffed full of air and god knows what additives. Besides, when someone gets interested in making bread in a bread machine, they get interested in bread, period. Haven't I started making my own from scratch once in a while when I have time?"

His wife laughed. "Don't be so defensive. I love you and your new hobby. It is more like a crusade, though, isn't it? Stand up tall and give your speech. Don't forget to smile once in a while. No bread baker will be able to resist you if you smile. Hurry now, before the kids get down here. We all have chores to do."

Ernest looked at his wife with pain in his eyes. "When you said kids it made me think again about the Akers and their loss." he said. "Children shouldn't pass before their parents. I don't think they will ever get over it."

"Benjamin was a wonderful young man. I just can't understand it. If it weren't Benjamin I'd think he'd been drinking or something worse. I guess we'll never know what made him run in front of that train."

Ernest nodded his head seriously. "God works in mysterious ways."

Patrick Sullivan gazed absentmindedly out his office window. It wasn't a pretty sight. The area around 31st and Main in Kansas City had been targeted for a big urban renewal project. Almost 100 acres of houses and businesses had been razed and then, because of the usual petty bickering on the city council and a major tenant backing out, the project had bogged down. A startlingly bare stretch of land lay smack dab in the middle of Kansas City. Patrick's employers, BIG BREAD, INC., had taken advantage of the confusion to pick up a square block close to the project and build a new research and development facility. It had cost them a third of what it would have to build the same project out in the suburbs, in Kansas. But it sat like a bunker in the desert right now. Acres of land stretched out behind the building, waiting. In front was Main Street, the major north-south artery that the name implied. As weird as it was to feel that way in the midst of a city, Patrick always felt alone when he looked out at this strip of Main Street in front of his office, despite the traffic passing by. There were no people on the streets.

A transplant from St. Louis, Patrick had the typical condescending St. Louis view of Kansas City when he arrived, and nothing had changed. He turned away from the depressing scene and back to his visitor. "So, did you wait until now to spring this on me because you knew I'd hate it? I do, you know."

The woman in the red power suit laughed nervously. "Why do you think my boss sent me with the bad tidings, instead of coming himself? He knew you wouldn't be thrilled. But we are the public relations department and this is necessary PR work. And it has been cleared all the way to the top."

Patrick sighed deeply. He arranged and rearranged the three loaves of bread that sat on top of his desk. He assumed they were something new the R and D team had left for him to try. "Why me?"

"Because you're the rising star of the research side of the company. These artisan bakers have given us nothing but grief since they started making waves in the bread world ten years ago. We are the enemy, and they're coming right into our camp, having their annual meeting here in Kansas City. We've got to meet them head on. They're sure to speak to the press and point to us as the bad guys, pumping bread full of air and chemicals. We need to show them we are doing research that will make our company more compatible with their stupid agenda. Plus you were a chef. You talk their lingo."

Patrick shifted uncomfortably. "Was a chef. Boy, you know how to hurt a guy. Which is exactly why I don't want to participate in this circus. I'll be the guy the crowds part for, the one they wear the garlic wreaths for."

"The one with the silver stake in your heart? Oh, please, you're a big boy. So they hate you. Big deal. I bet the most successful of them, someone like that Acme Bakery guy in Berkeley, doesn't make what you make now. And you're young, with lots of years of promotions ahead. What do you care what they think?"

Patrick saw a sliver of light, and he went for it. "My point exactly. We are the biggest bread manufacturer in the United States. What do we care what this group of zealots says about us? Why not just ignore them?"

The red power suit got up and Patrick sensed he had lost the argument. She paused at the door. "Ever since the Twinkie defense became a courtroom joke, our board has been very thin-skinned about our image," she said. "They want to buff it up and Patrick, you are the man of the hour to do that. Most people in this company would jump at the chance to take our case to the celebrity bread makers. Make us look good."

Patrick smiled weakly as she closed the door. The thick folder of information and suggestions from PR was smack in the middle of his desk.

"What am I doing here?" he asked himself out loud as he opened the file.

It was late afternoon in Düsseldorf. Dieter Bishop paced in the backroom of his bakery as his assistants packed the Styrofoam coolers. His bags sat by the door of the kitchen. He had insisted on waiting until the last possible moment to grind the flour he was taking with him to the United

States. He wanted it as fresh as possible. So Dieter paced while one of his assistants ground away in the little milling room at the back of the bakery. Custom flour was one of the things that made Dieter famous.

Paolo, his right hand man, was packing another cooler with the starter. Paolo had nursed this sourdough along for years now. It was like his child. "The Biga, she is ready for her trip," the man murmured gently, looking lovingly at a plastic bag filled only a quarter with dough and surrounded by blue freezer packs.

Dieter reacted to the other man's tenderness. "Why do you insist on calling it that?" he snapped.

Paolo shrugged and closed the lid, started taping it in place with strapping tape. "Because I'm Italian. That is what sour starter is called."

Dieter took the cooler impatiently away from the other man. "Don't brag about your heritage. You Italians are the ones who tried to make good bread without salt."

Paolo stood up and tried to defend himself and his country. "I've seen you eat many of my Tuscan loaves and not complain. And our customers buy plenty of them too."

Dieter's tense expression broke into a smile. "I'm a dummkopf today. I'm sorry."

Paolo held out his hand to his boss. "Good luck in Kansas City. I know you'll do a great job, and they'll love our bread. I wish I could go."

Dieter shook hands with Paolo, then embraced him and each of the workers lined up at the door to see him off. He smiled again. "I'm tired of those French bastards getting all the credit. Last year ARTOS had Poulaine as their key note speaker. This year it's my turn. I'm going to make them forget the word baguette."

"Speaking of bread, do you want to take a loaf with you

for the plane?" Paolo asked, grabbing one of the loaves that was sitting on Dieter's desk. They must have been left over from the day before. Dieter stuck the loaf under his arm absentmindedly.

Paolo picked up two of the coolers and started out the door behind Dieter. "Just remember boss, Pumpernickel rules."

Baked Eggs

10 eggs
2 cups all-purpose flour
2 ½ cups milk
2 T. sugar
1 tsp. kosher salt
1 T. vanilla
Confectioners sugar
Juice of one lemon

I first ate this wonderful egg dish under the name "Swedish Breakfast." The next time I ran into it, it was titled "Dutch Babies." Whatever the name, it is a great company brunch item. Be sure you can serve it straight out of the oven as it puffs up during baking, soon to lose its soufflé-like height.

Whip the eggs, milk and sugar together until frothy, either with a whisk or an electric mixer. Gently fold in the flour, mixing until there are no lumps. Add salt and vanilla.

Heat and spray with non-stick spray a medium-sized cast iron skillet or sauté pan. Pour batter in the heated pan and bake at 400 degrees for 15 minutes. Remove from oven and sprinkle with confectioners sugar and the lemon juice.

Three

It was almost eleven-thirty at night. Heaven pushed through the swinging door into the dining room and felt the coolness, her eyes adjusting to the dim lighting. It was a relief after the harsh lights and the heat of the kitchen. The open mike had been over since eleven, but the room was more than half full, mostly with drinkers, folks who had come out to see the collection of talent that had appeared on the stage on Monday night. The crowd was in high spirits. Joe Long and Chris Snyder, waiters and also the producers of the open mike nights, were headed toward Heaven. So was Murray Steinblatz, the doorman at Cafe Heaven on weekends and emcee on Mondays for the open mike. Heaven put her hands up over her head defensively. "I surrender already. Three of you all at once is too much."

Joe Long looked at Heaven slyly. "Then is this the right time to ask for two more microphones? Ours were old when we got them and they just don't sound good and . . ."

Heaven sat down at a bar stool with the trio hovering.

"Will you get me a glass of Cloudy Bay Sauvignon Blanc, please. It just came in yesterday, the new release," she said to anyone who might be listening behind the bar. She turned to Joe. "It's been a long time since we spent any money on our theatrical department, so if you do all the comparison shopping, I'll try to squeeze the money out of next month. The quarterly taxes are due this month so maybe next month we'll have a little extra."

Chris Snyder, left to play the good cop now that Joe had wheedled the new equipment out of Heaven, smiled and flounced his long blonde hair. "The show was good tonight. A whole group of poets came from the Writer's Place and read."

"So I heard, from my post in the peanut gallery, which is also known as the sauté station in the kitchen. It didn't seem to put the crowd to sleep, thank God." Heaven was always leery of a show with more than two poets.

Chris nodded his approval. "No, they were quite entertaining, actually. I told them they could come back every three months as a group. Some of them are already regulars as singles."

Joe broke in. "We can bill them as a pack of poets."

Chris ignored his friend. "There was a good video piece by the guy who's the head of the video department at the Art Institute."

Heaven sipped her wine. "It must have been. The crowd was whooping. Something we always like in a crowd, eh Murray? Murray, you sure are quiet tonight. What's the matter? Did they give you a hard time?"

Murray Steinblatz hitched up his pants nervously. As Murray journeyed into his fifth decade, his butt had disappeared along with anything that could be described as muscle tone on the rest of his body. Somehow it just made him more adorable. Always wiry, Murray was a bundle of nervous energy tonight. "No, no, Heaven. The crowd was great. They laughed at all my bad jokes and . . ."

Heaven eyed her friend. Something was up with Murray, that was for sure. "Did you get my message about Thursday? I want to go out on this field trip with the bread people, and I'd feel better if you would work that night. Actually, Iris and I are going to go out Wednesday evening and spend the night with my brother Del, at the farm. Iris hasn't been out there this summer, and we'll only be about ten miles from the first stop of the day Thursday. But I don't think you have to work Wednesday night," she paused. "And I don't think you heard a thing I just said."

Even if he hadn't been listening, Murray got the drift. "Sure, sure. I got your message and sure I'll work. No problem." Murray looked like he was dying to talk but nothing of substance came out. He shifted his trousers again and turned completely around, 360 degrees, and just stood looking at Heaven with a stupid look on his face. Heaven wanted to shake him, get him to spit out what was on his mind.

"That reminds me," Chris said. "Joe and I have a great idea for next Monday when all the bread people will be in town. You know how those craft people make stuff out of flour and water, well we were thinking . . ."

"Chris, Joe, can it," Heaven said with her eyes on Murray. "I'm tired and I don't want to hear about anything that the Health Department would disapprove of. Get lost. Check your tables. Better yet, go back and order me a pork tenderloin and a hot hacked chicken to go. I want to take something home to Iris and Hank."

"Iris and Hank? Are they at home together?" Joe asked anxiously.

Heaven was getting irritated. "So you think my twenty-two year old daughter and my twenty-six year old boyfriend can't be trusted together? Is that what you're implying?"

Joe looked frantically at Chris and Murray for a bail-out. They looked away. "Actually Hank is twenty-seven now, isn't he? I think at his last birthday . . ." his voice trailed off uncertainly. "I don't know where that came from. Iris has been home all summer. I'm sure they've spent lots of time together . . . I mean . . ."

Heaven drank her wine and glared at her friend. "Joe, I'm not about to help you out of this one. However, I have two things to say about this particular part of my life. One, I am the first to see that Hank should be more interested in my daughter if age is a determining factor. But after two years, I have concluded that the guy, for whatever reason, is crazy about me."

"Crazy about you, madly in love," Joe agreed.

Heaven went on. "Second point. As horrible as I would feel if Hank and Iris were attracted to each other, I would almost prefer it to who she is actually involved with."

Both Chris and Joe were dying to hear who that was, but Heaven didn't elaborate. She put her hand out to Murray. "Guys, like I told you, get lost. Murray, my man. Sit right down here and have a Diet Coke, your favorite. Tell mama what's on your mind."

Murray sat down and tried a weak smile. The bartender set a tall glass of cola in front of him. He didn't even take a drink. "Heaven, do you remember at the beginning of the summer when you and the boys went to Aspen?"

"How could I forget, Murray. I almost got pitched out of a ski gondola on Aspen Mountain."

"And Mona got stuck on the roof and Jumpin Jack

thought there were terrorists invading. Yes, sir. It was quite a five days, on both sides of Kansas."

Heaven patted Murray's hand. "But we came back alive, and you handled everything here, Murray. By the way, when will Jack get out of the hospital?"

"In a week or two. I talked to his doctor, and they think they have his medication under control. After how agitated he was in June, the doctors overreacted. They had Jack medicated like he weighed 300 pounds, and we both know he must be around 180. Poor Jack was sleeping twenty hours a day."

Murray had convinced their friend, no stranger to the psychiatric ward, to check himself in for observation. "Anyway, back to that weekend. I wrote a piece. And I read it at the open mike that Monday. It was about my fear of heights. But it was really about my fear of everything, since my Eva died. It was especially about my fear of having a life, like I don't deserve it. If she can't have a life, neither can I."

"And everyone said it was a great piece, Murray. I was hoping that it meant you were ready to write again. You ol' Pulitzer winner, you."

"That was a long time ago, babe. New York and the *Times*. I can't even remember how I did it. I just lost my chops, you know?"

"Murray, we've been over this before. You did not lose your chops. It's just like riding a bicycle or having sex. Didn't writing that piece show you that?"

Murray took a drink of his soda. His voice was shaky. "Yeah, it must have. Cause, I've been writing."

Heaven turned towards him. "And?"

"I've been writing a lot. Just about stuff here at the cafe

and around town. And its been sounding pretty good, so I finally called my old editor, who retired last year. He made some calls and . . . well . . ."

Heaven threw her arms around Murray's neck and planted a kiss on his cheek. "You're going back to the New York Tomes, I mean *Times.*"

Murray looked embarrassed and unwound himself from Heaven's embrace. "No, no, nothing like that. I took the name you came up with a few months ago when you were ragging me to get back to writing, 'Letters from the Interior.' I pitched writing something once a month, at least for now. And they went for it. I'm to send back dispatches from the front, in this case the Midwest, very colonial. They don't want to come out here themselves, of course, but they sell a lot of papers in the Midwest. They even have a reporter stationed in Kansas City, but he doesn't do any of the soft stuff."

"Yes, yes, yes," Heaven was bouncing up and down on her bar stool. Then she stopped, mid-bounce. "Then why are you acting like you lost your last friend for God's sake? Wait, you're not quitting, are you?"

"Oh, God, no. This place is my family, my home. This just happened today. I got the OK from the editor of the Lifestyle section, and I'm scared to death, H. I'm supposed to send a few things this week, just so they can get the feel. And now I look at the stuff and I just don't know. Would you mind reading over a few pieces? I know you've got the bread thing but I need your opinion."

Heaven got up and hugged Murray again. "I'm so proud of you. I know this takes more guts than I can even imagine. Drop some stuff off here tomorrow. I'm honored that you ask. And proud that I thought of the name of your new gig. We'll give 'em 'Letters from the Interior'. Now I'm going home before that four top in the corner sees me and I'm stuck here another hour. One of them called today and left a message on my machine at home, something about helping them with the big gala opening of the jazz area. It sounded like a lot of work to me. I want to get home now to my baby. Iris leaves in a week and I'm already freaking about it."

Murray got up too, and went back to his maitre d' mode. His eyes scanned the room as he walked Heaven towards the back where her van was parked. "You're sad because it's time for Iris to go back to England, to college. I guess once a Mom, always a Mom."

Heaven's eyes clouded over. "Yes, this year I'm dreading her going back. She only has this one last year, and I guess I'd hoped she could make it through without . . . Christ, I sound boring and totally predictable, a classic overprotective mother."

Murray wanted to draw Heaven out, but he figured they couldn't both have moments of truth the same night. Whatever it was, it probably wasn't as bad as Heaven thought. Iris was a terrific kid and seemed to have her head on her shoulders for someone whose dad was rock 'n' roll royalty. "Get out, babe. It's almost midnight. Don't forget your food. I see it up there in the kitchen window."

Heaven grabbed her to-go order and headed for 5th Street and home.

Heaven didn't live in the fashionable areas around the Country Club Plaza shopping center or a few blocks south in Brookside, the old fashioned neighborhoods with big, comfortable houses where many of her friends lived.

When she returned to Kansas City from London, pregnant with Iris, she discovered the Columbus Park area down by the river, an immigrant neighborhood that had been home to the Irish, the Italians, and by the time she moved in, the Vietnamese.

When Iris was a baby, their elderly neighbor on 5th Street died and left Heaven the building that was his home and also housed his business, a bread bakery. The bakery closed after Angelo Broncato died and soon Heaven and her baby moved in. Although she and Iris had lived with husbands in other places, she had always kept 5th Street.

Heaven thought of that now as she drove home. A space that had been a bread bakery had been her sanctuary, the one constant thing in a life of change. It was strange that it had taken her so long to become involved in making bread herself. The first floor of the bakery had evolved into a huge commercial kitchen and entertaining area when Heaven had been a caterer. She always kept the bread ovens and coal fire boxes exposed in the brick walls. And she continued the bread theme by using bakers racks to store all the platters and baskets that she used for food displays. But making bread, well, that was something she had never tackled until now.

Heaven had built a garage over the parking lot that had been provided for the bakery customers. As she pressed the garage-door opener, she saw that Iris was home, her beat-up pickup truck already parked. Hank's car was parked on the street; obviously he had been able to leave the hospital on time. Heaven was anxious and glad to be home. She went in the house and walked through the darkened kitchen and took the stairs to the rest of the living quarters on the second floor. She had knocked down walls upstairs to create big bedroom-studies for herself and Iris. What had been eight rooms when Angelo was alive was now just three, counting the huge bathroom with all kinds of trick showers and tubs.

Heaven had lots of collections: old photographs, quilts, 1950s lamps, Mission oak furniture. There were several massive overstuffed couches, lots of books and bookshelves, with every magazine known to man. It was cluttered but with stuff you wanted to look at, books you wanted to read. Hank called it a stimulating environment.

This summer had flown by. Iris had worked at the restaurant and written for a free newspaper. Heaven had enjoyed having her home at least for the first few weeks. Until Iris had told her about Stuart. Although Iris had still seemed to be having a good time, visiting high schools friends, writing and waiting tables, worry preoccupied Heaven. She thought she had carried on with modest success, not whining too often at her daughter to find a younger, more suitable beau. She could count on one hand the times she had lost her cool with Iris over the summer. But each time it had been about her daughter's new lover.

Now she stood in the doorway of Iris's suite and her cool evaporated, this time because she was faced with the reality of the end of the summer. Hank and Iris were sitting on the floor, surrounded by suitcases and empty boxes. Iris was packing to go back to Oxford, and that reality was almost too much for Heaven. Iris sat there, hair pulled up in a ponytail, showing Hank some photographs she had printed. Both Iris and Heaven had a taste for black and white photography and Heaven had rigged up a darkroom in the basement.

"Mom, you're finally home. How was the open mike? Did you bring us any food? We're starved," Iris said, seemingly without a care in the world.

Hank held up his hand to Heaven and she moved toward him. His eyes held understanding. He knew that Iris' leaving was painful for Heaven. "H, your daughter has an-

other skill. She has a great eye. Each frame is so complete."
Hank pulled Heaven down to the floor beside him and
gave her a kiss. She was choked up and didn't trust her
voice to not come out a croak. What's more, she was afraid
she would whine and grovel, never attractive attributes in
a mother. She could just hear herself begging Iris to stay in
Kansas City another week. So, instead of talking, she started
unpacking their midnight snack.

Iris was excited about her photos. "I got to shoot the
photos for this concert that I'm reviewing for the NEW
GRAPH. Its been fun, being a music reviewer. I guess
I hadn't thought about writing about rock. What with
Dad being so much a part of the music world, I've always
just been in the middle of it. But, of course, this new editor
for the GRAPH only saw me as Dennis McGuinne's daughter and naturally assumed I'd want to write about rock 'n'
roll."

Heaven smiled and got up to go downstairs and get
plates and silverware for everyone. "I was just thinking
about that tonight. Not you and rock music, but me and
bread. Same deal though. I have lived off and on in this
bread bakery since before you were born and I've never
been curious about learning to bake bread until now."

Hank looked at both of them. "Talk about the forest and
the trees. This could be the start of new interests for both
of you."

"I'll be right back, I'll get plates," Heaven said as she disappeared down the stairs. "Stay in the moment, woman,"
she scolded herself out loud as she rustled around the big
kitchen. "Don't spoil the time you have together worrying
about the time you don't have together."

She opened the refrigerator and took out a large bottle
of Chimay, the Belgian beer. Heaven didn't usually drink

beer but she knew both Hank and Iris liked this ale. She found a tray and loaded it with plates, cutlery, and glasses. Then she remembered something and went back to the refrigerator. She found half of a green tomato and apple pie that she had made on Sunday. September was a time when tomatoes were coming out of everyone's ears in Kansas City. Heaven had several plants in the alley behind the cafe. It was easy to pick some green for this tart pie.

Just as Heaven was getting ready to mount the stairs with her bounty, the phone rang. She picked up the kitchen phone, dreading a problem at the restaurant or worse, a call from the hospital where Hank was a resident, summoning him back to work. It was neither.

"Heaven, love, that you?"

Heaven felt the hairs on the back of her neck stand up. "Yes, Stuart, its me. What are you doing up so early? It must be the crack of dawn in England. Or haven't you been to bed yet?"

There was a hollow laugh from the other end of the line. "No, love, those days are long gone, except when we do the occasional concert, you know. Iris keeps me on the straight and narrow now. I can hardly wait for her to get back over here. Can I speak to the darling girl, Heaven?"

Heaven felt the bile rising in her throat. "Just a minute, Stuart," she put the phone on hold and took a deep breath. Then, trying hard to control the tone of her voice she called up the stairs, "Iris, the phone is for you." She sat down at the big table and listened to her daughter's delight when she picked up the call. Her laughter drifted down the stairs. Heaven held her breath, listening.

Suddenly Huy Wing, who was called Hank only by his Anglo friends and at the hospital, appeared beside her, his hand on her shoulder.

"Heaven, why do you disapprove of Iris and this Stuart being a couple?"

Heaven flared. "Oh, I don't know. Could it be that he's as old as her father, that he's a member of her father's band, her father's song writing partner, that he's the most notorious bass player and drug user and womanizer in the history of rock and roll? Could that have something to do with it? When Dennis asked if Iris could go to college in England I agreed because Dennis has always been a good father and he had cleaned up his act. Now I wish I'd never let her go."

Hank rubbed her neck soothingly. "Wait a minute. Stop right there. Has that changed? Hasn't Dennis been good to Iris? Hasn't he stayed clean?"

"Apart from the expensive French wine with dinner, he's sober as a judge," Heaven conceded.

"And hasn't Stuart cleaned up his act, too? And couldn't Iris have found a boyfriend you didn't approve of right here in Kansas City? The two things, Iris going to school in England and getting to be with her father, and her having a boyfriend you don't like, are unrelated."

"This isn't a *boy*friend. This guy has to be close to fifty." As soon as those words were out of her mouth, Heaven realized how ridiculous that must have sounded. After all, she was close to fifty and Hank, well, Hank wasn't. What was the difference? She kept quiet though, hoping Hank wouldn't bust her. Hank was too smart to let her get by with it.

Hank reached down and kissed Heaven's neck. She felt a rush of heat move down her body. "And what do we say about my mother and her reluctance to accept our relationship?" Hank asked softly.

Heaven felt the heat turn into a blush. Why did Hank always have to be so damn clear-headed? It was just like him to bring up his mother, to point out the similarities in the two situations. "We say she doesn't understand how real, how genuine, our feelings for each other are." Surely Stuart couldn't love Iris the way she loved Hank. She stood up and picked up the tray of plates and food and beer. "I can't help it. I know this guy too well. I don't want Iris to be . . ."

Hank took the tray from Heaven "Hurt? I have to speak up for Iris by telling you how I would feel. You are older than I am, yes. What would hurt me more? The chance of you breaking my heart or not being able to be with you at all? I can tell you I want to take my chances, and if Iris is in love so does she. No one can predict the future. I learned that the day I left Vietnam when I was four. Iris could just as easily break this Stuart's heart."

A happy voice yelled from upstairs, "Hey, where're the forks? I'm starving!"

Heaven followed Hank to the stairs. Or you could just as easily break mine, she thought. "So what you're telling me is, chill out?"

"What I'm telling you is I love you and yes, chill out."

Green Tomato and Apple Pie

Your favorite pie crust recipe, enough for a two-crust pie
1 cup sugar
¼ tsp. kosher salt
½ tsp. cinnamon
1 T. grated lemon zest
2 cups peeled, cored, and thinly sliced apple, 'Early
    Jonathan' or 'Granny Smith'
2 cups thinly sliced green tomatoes
2 T. lemon juice
½ cup sweet unsalted butter
1 egg white

Line your pie pan with dough. Combine sugar, salt, zest, and cinnamon. As you slice the apples, drop them in a separate bowl containing the lemon juice so they won't turn brown. Slice the tomatoes in a separate bowl. At this point you should have three bowls going, one with the sugar mixture, one with tomatoes, one with apples. Toss the apples with half of the sugar mixture, the tomatoes with the other half. Layer them in the pie pan and dot with butter. Place your top crust and brush with egg white. Bake for approximately 50 minutes in a 350 degree oven. Check it once in a while; it never hurts to turn baked goods halfway through the process in case your oven has a hot spot (most of them do).

Four

Patrick Sullivan reached in his bottom desk drawer for the bottle of cognac. Placed there for medicinal emergencies, Patrick knew this didn't exactly qualify as a life-or-death situation. He pulled it out anyway.

Going to the registration and opening reception for the bread conference had been a less-than-positive experience. Wherever he looked, there was a chef or baker he wanted to meet. When he went up and introduced himself and they saw his name tag, most would smile politely, say hello, and walk away. That was most. Then there was that woman from Chicago who flat out asked him how he had the nerve to show his face. He tried the old "we-have-to-feed-billions-of-people-on-this-planet-and-they-can't-all-afford-expensive-artisan-bread" line on her. She had countered with, "take some of those gross profits you make and help establish village ovens in third world countries. Poor people shouldn't buy bread, especially bread that isn't good for them," she said. "Poor people used to survive without BIG

BREAD and it would be better for everyone if they did again," she said.

Patrick had smiled and told her the village oven idea was a good one, that he would pass it on. In his hurry to get away from her, he turned and stumbled into a worse situation. Several of the ARTOS board members were in a huddle with some of the Kansas City host committee members. They were quite upset about the proposed tour of the BIG BREAD facility that was scheduled for Saturday afternoon. Why would anyone want to go into that den of iniquity, they asked. This was just the kind of bread that had ruined the country, that the ARTOS organization was out to eradicate, they said.

Having walked into this group, the Kansas City host committee members now looked at Patrick for some help. "Let me remind you ladies and gentlemen that you all have production issues in the course of creating your own hearth-style breads," Patrick had said cordially. "The Kansas City committee thought that it might be interesting to all of you to see how the largest bread manufacturer in the United States does it. After all, you came here to experience things you can't find in New York City."

That had mollified the snippy New Yorkers and had saved the host committee from humiliation. But Patrick could tell they hated him. All of them. In his former life, as a chef, he had always been judged for what he produced. It was *mano y mano*, something between you and the guest. Now he was the symbol of a whole company. He could be the nicest guy in Kansas City and they would still hate him for making white bread for the masses.

Patrick poured a heavy shot of cognac into his office coffee mug. It was after five o'clock. He could hear the exodus of the office workers outside his door. Patrick imagined them all going home to loving husbands and wives, well-mannered and intelligent children, clean and beautifully decorated homes. He was lonely. He had been married once, in college. He hadn't heard from his ex-wife in three or four years now, didn't even know if she was still in St. Louis.

His social life hadn't really jelled since his move to Kansas City.

"Okay, admit it," Patrick said out loud to himself after a big swig of cognac. "You were looking forward to being around real chefs again and they hate you for who you work for. You're going to be an outcast this weekend. Unless . . ."

Patrick Sullivan got up from his desk and paced around for a good twenty minutes, every so often getting something out of the file cabinet. Then he filled up his coffee mug from the cognac bottle again, grabbed his lab coat and the files, and headed out the door. "Maybe there's another way to skin this cat," he mumbled as he went down the hall towards the research and development lab.

Dieter Bishop couldn't wait to get to his room. The last twenty minutes of the reception had been the longest of his life. He knew everyone was trying to be nice, that they were all supposed to introduce themselves to the keynote speaker, but he could only feel his heart pounding a million miles an hour and hear the ringing in his ears. He tried to keep it straight, here was the famous baker from Berkeley, California, there was the one from upstate New York. Was the man who asked him to come and talk to students about rye sourdough from the Culinary Institute of America, or from Johnson and Wales?

Dieter threw his bags down on the bed and went into the bathroom. He turned on the cold water full blast and splashed his face.

The trip had been a nightmare. A two-hour layover at JFK airport in New York had turned into five hours. He had expected to be able to shower and rest before the reception. Instead he had staggered into the hotel and been snatched to a meeting room immediately by a host committee member. The opening reception was in full swing and the whole room swooped down on him.

Dieter threw himself on the bed for a moment, eyes closed. But that ringing in his ears could not be denied. He started searching through his bags. He was so tired by this time, he wasn't sure where he had put it. In a moment, he was in a frenzy, throwing clothes and toilet items everywhere. Finally he found his kit, wrapped in a sweater. He pulled the syringe out and fumbled with the rest of the equipment.

He must never wait this long again.

You haven't said a thing since Topeka, Mom. Everything alright?"

"Oh, you know, honey. It's just your Mom being corny."

Iris laughed. "You sure picked a good place for it, although those look like soy beans to me, not corn."

Heaven smiled weakly at the joke. "Your life has been going so well that I haven't had much to complain about, except the fact that you're going to college across the Atlantic ocean. But you've been doing great in school, you've started writing, which is what you want to do, you and your father have had a good time together, I was hard put to find a worry. So now that I have one . . ."

Iris interrupted, her voice sharp. "By that I guess you mean Stuart. Mother, my life is still great, even better with Stuart in it. I'm twenty-two, for God's sake. Its about time I fell in love. There are girls I went to high school with that are already divorced."

"I understand that, honey. Its just who you fell in love with that is giving me sleepless nights."

"I can't believe we're having this conversation. You, of all people, have no right to criticize my choice in boyfriends," Iris snapped in a combative tone.

Heaven was stung. Iris had never mentioned any particular dislike of one of Heaven's husbands. "If you weren't my daughter, I'd just say butt out. Who are you to judge? But you are my daughter. Have you been hating the men in my life all these years? You certainly are an accomplished actress if that's so," Heaven said quietly.

Iris softened a little but she wasn't going to back down entirely. "Mom, what do you think your Mom would have said if she had lived to see you marry five times?"

"Jesus, Iris. Where is all this coming from?"

"No, Mom. I mean it. Your Mom died in a car wreck when you were married to Sandy. He was your teenage sweetheart and judging from the photographs you had a storybook wedding. You married your high school boyfriend and you two went to college together. That's where your Mom left you. You haven't had to explain anything to a mother since then. I might not be here if you had."

Heaven smiled in spite of wanting to pout a little longer. "You mean you think my sensible Midwestern mother might have been opposed to me running off with a rock 'n' roll musician, getting married in a neon-lit wedding chapel in Reno?"

"I think enough said about that one, Mom. And then

there was Ian Wolff, the world's most wonderful painter, to hear him tell it."

Heaven was surprised at the tone of Iris's voice. "OK, I know you were little then, but I thought Ian was nice to you. Is there something you haven't told me?"

"Mom, you were such a chump when it came to Ian. Yes, he was as nice to me as can be. He was as nice to me as he was to you. He was, and I guess he still is, a great painter. And just as long as we hung on his every word and worshiped the ground he walked on, he loved us. But have I heard from him in the last ten years? Not once have I heard from him."

Heaven drove in silence for a while. Why was her first instinct to defend this man? She had been madly in love. She had hung on his every word. And he had run off with a Brazilian performance artist. Heaven had been so discombobulated after Ian left she had committed a felony and lost her law license. Not that she could blame him for that. She was a lawyer. She knew better. But she also was definitely not thinking straight at the time. That was Ian's fault. She guessed she would never stop pining for the man, but she knew what Iris said about him was true. He was an egocentric monster, very similar to Stuart Watts. She was dying to point this out but kept quiet. She looked over at Iris hopefully. "Surely you're not gonna tell me you didn't like Sol Steinberg? He sure did love you."

Iris smiled. "If Sol hadn't kicked the bucket, we'd still be a happy family. He was the greatest. The Sol years, in that big house in Mission Hills, the Sol years were fun."

"There just weren't enough of them. Poor Sol. He wasn't even sixty. Poor us."

"Yeah, it was back to 5th Street for Heaven and Iris," Iris said wryly.

Heaven grimaced. "One thing your Mom won't argue with you on. She was never good at getting their money. I ended up in the hole almost every time. Well, we're getting to the end of the list. What about Jason Kelley?"

"Mom, I was a teenager by then, and I didn't pay much attention. He was funny and very handsome and you two seemed to really like each other until you opened the restaurant. Then neither one of us saw much of you. But I understood. First, you have to make a living. You've been around Kansas City for a long time, and you were right to trade in on your 'fame' and try a restaurant. Second, I knew I'd be leaving for college. You had to take care of yourself. Jason didn't see it that way."

"Do you think I . . . no, I can't go back. Something happens along the way. Even if they offer to take care of you, and Jason did offer, you get gun-shy. You don't want to have to make up for lost time later."

Iris punched her Mom's arm. "If you had just had a better divorce lawyer over the years, you wouldn't have to work these long hours at the restaurant. Its a good thing Hank has long hours too."

"I'm afraid to hear what you have to say about Hank after this little session."

"Don't worry, Mom. Hank is too young to have many bad habits yet."

The two women laughed. Heaven wanted to go back and defend herself over all the men, all the mistakes, all the history. She touched her daughters arm. "Was it horrible for you? I always just went doggedly ahead, one foot in front of the other. Was it just terrible?"

Iris shook her head and seemed to be examining her lap. "There were times when I wanted the perfect family, with a Mom and a Dad and a brother or sister and a dog.

But you and Dad both did a good job of making me feel loved and that's the bottom line." Iris folded her arms. "But Mom, do you see? I wasn't making you relive the past just to be mean. I'm sure you had a very good reason for each one of those relationships. I have a very good reason for Stuart. I love him. I went along for the ride with you. Now you have to do the same for me."

Heaven took the Council Grove exit off I-70. They were driving into the late afternoon sun, so Heaven had to watch what she was doing. As they turned down a county road, heading for the farm where Heaven grew up, Iris cleared her throat. "Mom, there's one more thing. Now is as good a time as any to talk about it."

Heaven looked at her daughter in horror. "You're not pregnant, are you?"

"Mother, please. Of course not. I have no intention of having kids for ages. And I've been here all summer so if I were pregnant with Stuart's child you would have known it long ago. No, its just that when I finish Oxford, I don't plan to come back to Kansas City to live. And this isn't something that is dependent on Stuart. Even if we aren't to-gether next spring, I'm not coming back."

Heaven was sick at heart. She had feared this. "Will you stay in England?"

"I don't know right now. If I want to write for magazines I should go to New York. I know I don't want to do the daily newspaper thing. If I wanted that I should have stayed here and gone to MU at Columbia. They have one of the best journalism schools in the world. If I want to try to write novels . . . well, I just want you to know that Kansas City isn't on the short list. And that doesn't mean that some day . . ." Iris trailed off, exhausted all of a sudden. She had been dreading telling her mother about this, as much as she had dreaded telling her about Stuart. Now it was done, and she just wanted to take a nap. Stress always made her sleepy.

Here they were, driving down a two-lane highway to the farm Heaven was born and raised on. Even if her parents hadn't died in a car accident, Heaven couldn't imagine coming back here to live. She loved the place. It held good memories. But it had never crossed her mind that she could live out here. "I guess you feel the same way about Kansas City that I feel about this farm," Heaven said as she pulled onto the gravel road that was the final leg of the journey.

Goldenrod and Queen Anne's lace bloomed all along the road. A hedgerow of tall bushes protected the road from the Kansas wind that could blow snow into high drifts. Heaven saw 'Suffolk' sheep, 'China Poland' pigs, a couple of 'Jersey' cows. Del, Heaven's brother, said he didn't mind getting up to milk them early in the morning, that their rich milk and cream were worth it, and he needed to get up anyway. Now that Del's kids were out of the nest, Heaven wondered what they did with all that milk. There was the house, with the big wraparound front porch. There were rattan rockers sitting out there, and a sturdy oak porch swing. It looked like Del had put a new red roof on the house this summer.

Iris looked around. "I don't know how you feel about your childhood home, Mom, but I love Kansas City. It's just not where I want to live."

"I know, I know. I don't want to be on the farm either, honey. But it sure has lots of sweet memories." Heaven pulled the van up under a big cottonwood tree next to the the drive. Del's pickup was parked near the house.

Iris stretched her arms, cramped from the drive. "What I remember about our trips out here were getting to ride a horse and Uncle Del's cows at the feed lot. Boy, did they stink. And I remember going to those farm sales that you love so much. They took all day."

"But we got some great stuff, didn't we? That harvest table that you did your homework on, and those dishes with the cattails, and all those old postcards, they were from that farm down by Cottonwood Falls." Heaven had perked up. She was walking toward the house eagerly now. How lucky to still be able to go to the house you grew up in and visit. She was bounding ahead of Iris, who was trailing behind, lugging their overnight bags. "I wonder what Debbie's got out in the barn," Heaven wondered out loud as she walked to the back door.

What did you think of that Beringer Knight's Valley Merlot?" Heaven asked. "It's allocated to the max. We only got six bottles for the whole vintage, and I wanted you to taste it." It was long after dinner, but no one wanted to get up from the table.

Del held up his empty glass. "Thanks for sharing the wealth. And I've got something I think you'll like." He got up and went over to a carved sideboard, and brought out a bottle and some small glasses. "This is a 1994 Taylor Fladgate vintage port. You know it got a perfect score in the *Spectator* when it was released. Enjoy."

Heaven smiled as her brother poured some for the four of them. "You've become quite a wine snob, bro. I hope I've been somewhat responsible."

Del gave a little tip of the glass to his sister. "Just because we're down on the farm, doesn't mean we don't like French burgundy and vintage port. Boy, this is good stuff."

Iris was still eating, tucking into a second piece of lemon

56

meringue pie. "Debbie, that was the best beef stew I've ever tasted," she said as she munched happily. Debbie, Del's wife, yelled her thanks from the kitchen. She had finally, reluctantly gone in to load the dishwasher. Del and Debbie's children were both in college. Their daughter was in law school in Chicago and their son was taking agribusiness at K-State.

Del looked at Heaven. "Well, I've heard all Iris's news. Now, what's going on with you, sis? What's this bread conference you're a part of? I heard something about it from my neighbor. But there's always some group coming out here for something or other. I can't keep them all straight. Last week it was a bunch of fancy architects who were here to look at the old limestone farm buildings. Said we had some of the best in the country. The week before, it was a bunch of German cattle farmers, came to the feedlot."

Del ran a cattle feedlot near Alma, about fifteen or twenty miles away from the farm, the places that cattlemen sent their herds to get them fattened up before sale. He had a manager for it, but he still had to go over three or four times a week. Del had days as long as Heaven's.

"Del, it sounds as though Kansas is staging a comeback. Next thing you know, people will be coming here on vacation, it'll be like a farm theme park," Iris teased.

Del grinned at his niece. "Oh, I don't think we have to worry about that. There was somethin' in the Topeka paper about how Kansas is the last state in preference for tourists. Heaven, I hear you're going to visit Walter Jinks in the morning. Now there's a strange case."

"Like how strange?" Heaven asked.

"Well, farmers are not the most liberal bunch, as you probably remember. If you'd asked me ahead of time, I'd have put a fella that led the peace movement at the bottom of the list of those that would fit in around here. Walter is a good neighbor. Even with all his theories about this perennial polyculture. But he has his detractors and his enemies, that's for sure."

"Perennial what? Enemies why?" Heaven asked.

Del grinned. "I don't want to spoil it for you, and Walter can tell it better, but it has to do with all this topsoil erosion that we've got, among other things. The enemies don't want to think about some of the possibilities for the future, how it could affect Kansas. This group of bread folks, they gonna be interested in Walter's far-out notions?"

Heaven smiled a smile that said, we're cool, we know about topsoil. "This isn't your run-of-the-mill white bread manufacturers. These are the owners of restaurants and bakeries that are trying to bring back old, European hearth bread-making methods. They chose Kansas City for their conference so they could see where wheat grows, touch it, stuff like that. I guess no one at ARTOS remembered that the wheat wouldn't be in the fields in September, but no one consulted this Kansas girl before they set up the conference for this time of year. The theme is 'Back to the Earth,' or something like that. Walter sounds right up our alley."

"Well, he's famous for it, I will say that. He got one of those McDowell grants, the ones they call the genius grants, where you get lots of money just for being who you are already," Del said.

Just then, the doorbell rang. "I bet that's Ernest Powell. He's having your bunch over for lunch tomorrow, and he needed to borrow some long tables. We've got plenty out in the barn," Del explained as he went to the door and opened it. A tall, gangly man with the red neck and rough hands of a farmer stood there, wearing a flat brimmed hat that Heaven recognized as the Mennonite style. Del shook his hand and the other man smiled shyly. "Ernest, this is my sister, Katherine. She goes by the name Heaven, but I reckon you'd think that was blasphemous, so you can call her Katy, like I used to. This is her daughter Iris."

Ernest stepped into the room gingerly, as if he were afraid he would break something. "It must be hard to sin with a name like that," he said with a twinkle in his eye.

Heaven got up from the table. "I wish that had been the case over the years, Mr. Powell. Del tells me you're going to be our host for lunch tomorrow. I'm a member of ARTOS, the bread group that's coming out to take a tour."

Ernest looked at Heaven with renewed interest. "That's right. Now I remember. You have a cafe in Kansas City?"

"Yes, I do."

"Well, I've been doing some baking, lately. I joined your group myself. Bread is sure a blessing," Ernest said. He looked like he wanted to sit down and visit, but he didn't.

As Del pulled on his boots he remembered his manners. "Say, Ernest, I'm real sorry about the Aker's boy." He turned to explain to Heaven and Iris. "One of Ernest's neighbors was killed by a run-in with a train."

Ernest's open face clouded over. "Thank you for that. Ben's folks are really tore up. I better get those tables and get home. Everyone is having a fit over at my house, cooking for such a bunch as you."

"Are you making . . ."

"Mennonite fare, yes ma'am," Ernest said, nodding to Iris and Heaven. He and Del went out the kitchen door.

In a few minutes, Del came back in, a smile on his face. "You just met the national bread-machine bread-making champion."

Heaven looked up from her glass of port. Iris was sipping

hers now, having finally taken her empty dessert plate to the kitchen. "Wait a minute," Iris said. "I thought Mennonites didn't have electricity? How can he be the bread-machine champ?"

Heaven shook her head. "I think that's Amish, right Del?"

Del nodded. "Amish don't have anything to do with mechanical gadgets or things that take fossil fuels to run. Mennonites may be like that in some other parts of the country, but these Kansas Mennonites, they went along with the rest of us when it came time to use a tractor instead of a team of horses."

"You know," Heaven spoke carefully, not wanting to sound too much like a food snob, "these bakers aren't exactly the bread-machine type. Most of them won't even use prepared yeast. They put out crushed grapes and collect wild yeasts, things like that."

Del chuckled. "I kinda figured that. But I'll tell you, Ernest is a real cheerleader about this. He thinks the bread machine is a gift from God to bring families back together again. He has a big plan to ask your group to buy a bunch of the dad-blame things and give them to poor folks. Says he's asking to be heard by the bunch at your big meeting."

"What a great idea," Iris said brightly. "They should do it."

"Yeah," Heaven said reluctantly. "It is a good idea. But I just hope this group is more openminded than I think they are. I'd hate for Ernest to be, you know, made fun of."

"Ernest is real serious about this. He'll be like a dog with a big bone. Until he gets what he wants, he won't let go. And don't worry about Ernest, he can handle himself fine," Del said as he took off his boots. "I'm beat, and we all have to get up early. I'm going to watch the ten o'clock news in bed." He gave Heaven a big hug and kissed Iris on the top of the head. "Night, sis. I think Deb has already beat me up the stairs."

Debbie yelled "good night all" from above. Iris got up. "Are you ready to go up to your old room, Mom? We'll be roomies in your old twin beds."

Heaven thought about her room and those matching candlestick beds. Del's daughter had used that room too. "Not yet, honey. I have to read these columns of Murray's." Heaven's voice was tentative. She put her hand on Iris's arm. "As much as I hated hearing you say you wouldn't move back to Kansas City, I can't say I was surprised. I'm glad we had that talk in the car. I'll try to keep my mouth shut about Stuart, like you have over the years about my men."

Iris hugged her mother's neck. "Stuart is wonderful, Mom, and so are you. Night, night, sleep tight and . . ."

"Don't let the bed bugs bite," Heaven said, her heart aching. The first time she'd heard that saying it had been in this house. It seemed like a million years ago. She got out Murray's articles and started her homework, pencil and post-its in hand.

Walter Jinks finished putting the last dishes away. Most of the interns and graduate students were spending the night at the farm, including the young lady he was currently sleeping with. They had all enjoyed a lively supper, vegetable lasagna, a big salad, and a bigger argument about a new soybean clone that all the Iowa farmers were crazy about. Then everyone had drifted off to the mill or the library, which would be the living room in a more conventional household.

There were five bedrooms in this big, old farmhouse, plus a guest cottage that Walter had fashioned out of an old stone out-building. That was plenty of room for all the students since his wife had left and their two children were grown and off on their own. Walter thought of his wife fondly, as always. He certainly couldn't blame her for growing tired of their way of life, constantly trying to raise enough money for the next year's experiments. She had finally taken a professorship at an agriculture college in Texas, using her botany degree and all she had learned with Walter.

Walter had discovered the foundation officers that liked to come investigate his projects, loved having a separate guest house to stay in. Walter had equipped it with a fax and an extra telephone line so they could hook up their laptop computers to the Internet. The more comfortable the foundation and trust boys were, the better chance Walter had of getting some of their money.

It wasn't easy trying to sell agriculture to these guys. Medical research, crack babies, help for single mothers, software, all were more popular places to put your dollars. Even culture: experimental theater, ballet, or supporting the local symphony were easier sells.

It had been so long since most folks in America were connected to where their food came from, no one even thought about it any more. The agriculture community had been too successful, that was the problem. Folks in a large city like Atlanta, say, read in the newspaper that the wheat crop in Kansas was wiped out by violent rainstorms, but the loaf of bread still cost fifty cents at the Kroger. How bad could it be?

Walter knew what was going to have to happen before the country would understand. An agricultural disaster was going to have to happen. And he could see several coming in the next few years. He just hoped the death toll could be kept to a minimum. That's why these celebrity bakers were so crucial. When they talked, people listened, people that read *Gourmet* magazine, not the obscure journals Walter wrote for.

Walter glanced at his watch. It was ten-thirty. The house was getting quiet. Everyone wanted a good night's sleep so they would be sharp for the tour tomorrow. He thought wistfully about the pretty red-head waiting for him in his bed. She would fall asleep soon and not know how much longer she slept alone. Walter got his tool bag out of the closet and made sure he had some gloves along. It was time for him to go to work. Quietly, he went out into the Kansas night.

Heaven fumbled around, looking for the light switch in the barn. After she finished her reading assignment, she still wasn't tired, though it was close to midnight. She had been "walking the property," as her Dad used to put it. When her Dad used that term, he meant looking for a broken fence, new weeds in the soybeans, a lamb that had escaped its designated pasture. Heaven had just been wandering aimlessly on the little path that led from one out-building to another. Now here she was in the barn.

When her folks were alive, her Mom had used the barn for an antique business. The hay was stored in an old farmhouse further out on the property, the animals had their own stable. The barn had more important things to do.

Heaven had even had her own little business when she was a teenager. She bought and sold old jukeboxes, before they had become the pricey collectibles they were today. In her house in Kansas City was an old Wurlitzer that she bought when she was fifteen. She'd been offered thousands for it but she wouldn't dream of selling it. It was some connection to her folks, her childhood.

Heaven's parents died coming home from an auction in Iowa. A semi driver fell asleep and crossed into the wrong lane of traffic, right into her folks and their van full of antique dolls. Her mother had specialized in antique dolls. In fact, Heaven had a broken doll, with violet glass eyes that were very unusual, that she had picked out of the boxes of debris from her parents' wrecked van. It sat by her bed and Heaven felt a little of her mother's spirit watching over her.

When Del and Debbie took over the farm, Debbie wanted to continue the antique business, and she'd done a great job. Her shop was a must-stop for antique nuts from Kansas City when they went out on a westward shopping trip. Debbie didn't do too much with dolls, though. She dealt in Mission style furniture, quilts and other fancywork, and kitchen collectibles, things that Heaven collected because of Debbie. Heaven had accumulated lots of good stuff for her catering business from Debbie over the years, antique silver, china serving pieces, beautiful glassware.

Tonight Heaven walked slowly around the barn, looking at the long tables covered with items like antique potato mashers and embroidered kitchen towels that had the days of the week and the appropriate chore for each day depicted in cross stitch. Each object brought back some little memory. Didn't Aunt Gert have towels like this? I remember Daddy using one of these apple corer things. Heaven picked up and put down a dozen items, each one touching off a remembrance.

Heaven was an emotional mess. The talk with Iris had

called up doubts about her own actions through the years. Then to top it off, she was at her childhood home. It was like the memories of every past mistake had jumped to the surface right under her skin and were itching to get loose. "If you had any sense, you'd get out of here right now, go in to bed," she said sternly out loud to herself.

She walked over to a wicker rocking chair and plopped down instead. Most days, Heaven kept her eyes on the road and took one step at a time, and most days it worked. Sometimes the past caught up though, and when it did, you were lucky if you could find a rocking chair to collapse in and meet those private demons. Heaven started rocking and crying. It felt great.

Borscht

Borscht is the cassoulet of Eastern Europe. By that, I mean each country, and I suspect, city, has its own version of this soup. The real origin of borscht seems to be the Ukraine in the 14th century. This is my hybrid, a version somewhere between the Mennonites of Kansas and the Ukraine. The thing to remember is to balance the sweet(beets, tomatoes, sugar) with the sour (vinegar or lemon juice). You want to be able to taste both sweet and sour as well as all the richness of the meat and the complexity of the vegetables cooked together.

Stock
2 lbs. beef chuck roast on the bone
1 ham hock
2 beef marrow bones
1 gal. water
1 onion, split with the skin on
1 carrot, washed but not peeled
2 ribs celery with leaves if available
1 parsnip, peeled if the outside has been waxed
Several dill sprigs
4 bay leaves
6 parsley sprigs

Soup

2 large beets

2 leeks, sliced and soaked in cold water for 20 minutes, then rinsed and drained

1 16 oz. can plum tomatoes

1 small can tomato paste

2 lbs. small potatoes, diced

4 cups red cabbage, shredded

2 'Granny Smith' apples, peeled and diced

2 parsnips, peeled and diced

2 carrots, peeled and sliced

1 turnip, diced

1 celery root, peeled and diced

2 cups white beans, cooked (optional)

4 cloves garlic, minced fine

Kosher salt, freshly ground pepper, sugar, lemon juice, apple cider vinegar

Finely chopped parsley, chopped fresh dill

Sour cream

Using cold water, combine all the stock ingredients in a large stock pot and bring to a boil, skimming foam occasionally. Reduce heat and simmer two hours, adding another quart of water if necessary. Strain the stock into a clean pot. Reserve the beef and ham hock and discard the rest.

While the stock is cooking, roast the beets. This gives them a tremendous concentration of flavor. Just wash them and leave the skin on. Put beets in a shallow baking dish and sprinkle with kosher salt and olive oil. Roast in a hot oven, 425 degrees, until the beets are fork tender. This could take as long as an hour or more depending on the size of the beets. Cool, pull the skins off, and dice.

Now you have a pot of strained stock and some cooked beets and lots of prepped vegetables. Heat the stock to simmer and put the celery root, leeks, potatoes, turnips, carrots, and parsnips in the stock. Let it simmer for fifteen minutes then add the cabbage, apples, and garlic. Simmer another fifteen minutes then add the tomatoes, tomato paste, beets and beans. Simmer another fifteen minutes, then start the seasoning process. I usually start with 1 T. each kosher salt, sugar, lemon juice, and vinegar. Note that I didn't salt the stock originally. When you have the balance of sweet and sour that suits your taste buds, cut the reserved beef and ham into bite size pieces and add to stock. Let the whole thing stand at least an hour to let the flavors marry, then re-season with salt, pepper and any additional sour you think it needs. Bring back to a boil, then serve hot with a dollop of sour cream, dill, and parsley on each serving for garnish. As it makes so much soup, this is a great dish to prepare, portion out in bags, and freeze.

Five

Ernest Powell came down the stairs to the kitchen. This morning there was no smell of fresh-baked bread from his bread machine. There were, however, six neighbor ladies all talking at once.

His wife smiled sweetly. "Ernest, you can take the kids to school, can't you? We missed the bus, what with all the chores to do this morning. They're outside putting the cloths on all the tables."

Ernest kissed his wife on the cheek. She blushed and so did several of her friends. "Of course, I'll take them in town. But won't those tablecloths blow away? You gals are getting ahead of yourselves."

"Oh, your son thought of that," Betsy Powell said proudly. He's got a rock on each corner and a few in the middle for good measure. Those table cloths aren't going anywhere."

Ernest poured himself a cup of coffee. "How did we get mixed up in this conference anyway?"

"Look who's talking, the famous bread maker himself,"

Betsy said. "Remember, when the committee members from Kansas City came out to see Walter about him giving a tour. . . ."

Ernest grinned. "I know, I know. Walter mentioned it at the grocery store and I couldn't get over there fast enough the next day. Walter's not the only one with an agenda."

His wife tucked his shirttail down in his jeans in the back. Then she turned him around and snapped his suspenders. "So you volunteered your wife and her church group to cook lunch for a bunch of chefs that have their recipes in all the magazines. Thanks so much."

Ernest put his coffee cup down. "Well, they gave us ten dollars a head for lunch, and if I know you all, you did it for four or five. That gives you some money for your church Christmas fund. And these fancy bakers will have the best lunch they've ever had, for any amount of money."

"Don't try to sweet talk, me, Ernest Powell. You get now, or the kids will be late for school."

Ernest paused at the kitchen door. "I'm heading over to Walter's for the tour. I'm curious what old Walter is up to these days. Ladies, I do thank you so much. I know you're going to wow them." Ernest stepped out and smiled. God had made a beautiful morning. "Kids! Let's go. Last one in the truck has to drive."

It was early but they were lost. Iris and Heaven were on a gravel road looking for the sign to the Grains Research Institute for Peace, GRIP for short.

Iris was the lookout. "If I didn't know better, I'd think Kansas was just one vast experimental farm. So far we've gone past signs to the Kansas State University experimental farm, the Extension Service experimental farm, and the

Soil Conservation Service test soil plots. What in the heck is all this experimenting?"

Heaven looked smug, "Well, because I'm on the host committee for this conference, I went to the Board of Trade last week and saw my friend David Gibbs, to set up the tour and all. I watched this fascinating film, all about buying long and selling short, soybean clones, and white winter wheat. Agriculture has become very big business, honey. I don't think these bakers have any idea what happens before they get their sacks of King Arthur."

"And what, pray tell, is King Arthur? Oh, Mom, there's the sign for GRIP. Turn left, and what's the peace allusion in the name?" Iris asked.

Heaven turned the van and raised a cloud of dust. "King Arthur is a popular high-gluten bread flour. The flour and wheat biz is just as boutique and trendy as other parts of the food business. We beat the buses from Kansas City." She parked the van under a shade tree and looked around. Near a limestone building a group of men and women were standing around talking. One of them, a middle-aged man with a shock of silver hair, waved and broke away from the crowd, heading for Heaven and Iris. "As for the peace part, Walter Jinks was a very famous peacenik who was one of the organizers of the big March on Washington during the Vietnam war," Heaven explained as they got out of the van. "Now he thinks he can bring about world peace by fixing agriculture. Or something. I'm sure we'll hear the whole story soon."

Iris pointed to a large cloud of dust coming their way. "We didn't beat them by far. That must be the buses."

Walter Jinks reached them first. "I happen to know that you're Heaven Lee," He said with a twinkle in his eye. "I've eaten in your restaurant several times when I've passed through Kansas City, and I've seen you bustle around the dining room. I also know your brother. Good man, Del."

Heaven reached out her hand and shook Walter's. "This is my daughter Iris McGuinne. We spent the night at Del's last night. That's why we beat the rest of the group. Del says you won a genius grant last year. A belated congratulations."

Walter smiled. "I figured it out. The prize, and I do appreciate it, believe me, averages out my income to about $27,000 annually for the last twenty years."

Heaven nodded. "And that means there were some mighty lean years. Well, I can hardly wait to learn what your research has produced. I hope those lean years are behind you now."

Walter's face had a very serious expression. "The work is far from over, Heaven. Excuse me while I go greet the rest of the guests," he said and walked toward the buses that had just pulled up and stopped in the drive.

Heaven watched as face after famous face climbed down the steps of the two big coaches. There must have been close to a hundred people descending, many of them cookbook authors and bakery owners and pastry chefs from well-known restaurants. At that moment, Pauline swooped out of bus number two, laughing and talking with someone Heaven recognized vaguely. Pauline spotted Heaven and Iris and headed their way. Heaven was glad to see that Pauline, usually a little shy, was openly having fun.

"How was the trip?" Heaven asked.

"Did you see who I was talking to?" Pauline asked. "That's one of the two women who started that bakery in Santa Fe last year. They were featured in *Food and Wine* last month."

Iris giggled. "Pauline, surely you're not a groupie?"

Pauline giggled back. "Every bus seat had someone sitting in it that was famous, to a baker at least. Either I had read their cookbook or seen them on the Food Channel. Is this what it's like when you go to a party at your Dad's house, celebrities everywhere?"

Iris rolled her eyes. "They're just Dad's buddies. No big deal."

Heaven was tickled that to Pauline, Noel Comiss from Top Hat Bakery in New York was as much a star as Keith Richards.

One of the GRIP graduate students walked by asking them to come over for a short presentation. The whole crowd was moving toward rows of metal folding chairs next to the house.

Heaven glanced at her watch. It was almost nine-thirty. "What time did you have to leave Kansas City, the crack of dawn?" she asked Pauline.

Pauline smiled. "Remember, H, this group is used to getting up early. We left at seven-thirty from the hotel. They had a portable espresso machine in each bus and bagels and stuff. It was fun."

Soon the whole group was assembled more or less where they were supposed to be. Walter Jinks also had coffee available, in a big stainless steel percolator on a card table. Heaven and Iris had just filled up two Styrofoam cups when Walter Jinks walked to the head of the group and clapped his hands together to get their attention.

"I want to welcome you to the Grain Research Institute for Peace. I'm going to talk briefly—and my students will tell you how rare that is—about what we do here and then we'll take a tour of some of the fields. I know your time is limited and that you're also touring the Studies Laboratory up in Manhattan." Walter's voice changed tenor, suddenly there was a bitter edge to it. "You couldn't visit two more different facilities in one day." He looked as if he were going to say more but changed his mind. As he talked he started walking slowly around the crowd.

"I want to change the world and I need you to help me. You see, Ernest Powell here, and his relatives, altered the course of civilization." Heaven was surprised to see the tall farmer sitting in one of the front rows. He must have arrived when she was talking to Pauline. Walter had stopped right in front of him and was pointing dramatically at Ernest. Ernest shifted in his chair and blushed. "In 1874, the first Mennonites came from Russia to Kansas to escape religious persecution. With them they brought 'Red Turkey' winter wheat, a strain from the Black Sea. Who could predict that it would grow so abundantly here on the North American prairie?" Walter asked. "It has grown too well. We have done our job as the breadbasket to the world too well. And because of it, through erosion we are losing tens of millions of acres of cropland every year. We are poisoning the North American continent with salts left in the fields from fertilizers, pesticides, and irrigation. And ironically, the more damage we do, the higher our production soars, at least for now." Walt's voice boomed with the delivery of a good Southern Baptist minister.

Heaven looked around. He had the crowd in the palm of his hand and he was going to bring it on home. "But it can't go on forever. Long after we have reached bedrock here on this prairie, our topsoil gone, long after we have used up all the fossil fuels and the airplanes and automobiles are rusting and silent, human beings will still need their daily bread. Perhaps then, sustainable agriculture will be a priority with the world powers." Heaven realized that she had never really seen farms and farmers in such exalted light before, as an indication of how history was going. The pros sitting around her had obviously realized agriculture's importance, however, even if Heaven hadn't. Their eyes shone with some sort of religious zeal.

Walter was preaching to the choir. "There are two ways to solve this dilemma," he said. "And they both involve herbaceous perennial seed-producing cultures. Yes, perennials instead of annuals, such as wheat and corn. Oh, we could breed these annuals that we know and love to be perennials. But have we really solved the problem? Don't we still depend on monoculture agriculture and the dangers that it represents? We used to have dozens of strains of wheat cultivated in the United States. Now there are only six, with 'Red Turkey' wheat by far the most prevalent. What if 'Red Turkey' wheat develops a disease fatal to its strain? How will we feed America then, much less the world?

"Instead of depending on this doomed monoculture, twenty-five years ago I began work on the second way, which is to develop native grasses and grains to be planted side by side and harvested together, a natural granola right from the fields. It is the way nature designed this prairie around us right here in Kansas, a polyculture. And this is where you come in. You are the most influential bakers in this country, indeed as I recognize some of our European guests, I would say the world. I ask you to taste the breads that my staff has prepared for you today, and to take the ten-pound sacks of our special perennial polyculture flour home with you. Please feel free to call us for more samples when you get home. We must break the tyranny of wheat domination!" Walter ended with a bang, glaring at Ernest Powell as if he had singlehandedly ruined the universe.

Out of the back of the farmhouse came several students with baskets of various styles of bread created with Walter's grain and grass combinations. There were regular leavened bread and flat breads. The flat breads, resembling home-made lavoosh, looked appealing to Heaven. Everyone rushed the tables to get a taste. There were also big chunks of butter and some jams that looked homemade. Soon gallon jugs of apple cider appeared. Walter was surrounded by bakers who spotted a new trend. They all wanted to be the first on their block to create a perennial polyculture loaf. Heaven, Iris, and Pauline moved around Walter to get some samples. They ate in silence for a minute, then Iris spoke first. "Well, I hope I'm dead and buried before we have to start eating this all the time."

Heaven chuckled. "Just slather some of this farm butter and 'Damson' plum jam on it. It's not so bad, and even if it is, these celeb bakers will be able to make something good out of it. These cracker ones are better than the raised breads. The raised breads are kind of heavy. Maybe they need more yeast."

Pauline was taking this taste test very seriously. Heaven was already planning to hide their complimentary sacks of Walter's flour when they got back to the restaurant. "The problem is . . ." Pauline started.

She was interrupted by a handsome blonde man. "The problem is that only wheat flour has the gluten that gives bread the light texture that we love," the hunk said in English heavy on the German accent. All three women batted their eyes instinctively. "God knows I have struggled with this problem myself for years. The rye flour does not have any gluten to speak of. Left by itself, it gives a heavy, lifeless loaf."

Pauline's eyes shone with recognition. "Now I know who you are. You're our keynote speaker, Dieter Bishop. You won the Coupe du Monde last year." She turned to Iris. "The Coupe du Monde is *the* bread competition in Europe."

Dieter tipped his head to the side, assessing all three women as if they were pastries in a Vienna coffee house. "And who might I have the pleasure of discussing this most important subject with?"

Heaven wondered if the important subject Dieter meant was the decline and fall of wheat versus rye or his recent success on the bread-contest circuit. She gave him the benefit of the doubt and assumed he wasn't totally self-absorbed. "I'm Heaven Lee, Dieter. This is my daughter, Iris McGuinne, and this is Pauline Kramer, the pastry chef and baker for my restaurant in Kansas City."

"Ah, yes," Dieter said, taking each hand in turn for a quick Prussian bow. "And do you cook or bake bread, or are you a front of the house owner?" he asked Heaven.

"I cook," Heaven said. "And I've just started trying to learn bread making, so I am all too familiar with the key role gluten plays in this whole sordid story." Dieter and Pauline looked at her uncomprehendingly. A sense of humor about their occupation did not seem to be a trait of bread bakers.

Iris rescued them. "It's just a joke. Mom doesn't think bread is sordid. Let's go get on one of those flatbed trucks for the tour, shall we?" she said hoping to move things along. It was getting hot out here in the fields. Iris was ready for the next stop on the tour and she hoped it was lunch.

As they walked to the trucks, Dieter and Pauline deep in talk about lipids in bread, Heaven punched Iris on the arm and pointed. "Speaking of sordid stories, it looks like

Ernest didn't like the one painted by Walter." The two men were in a heated conversation, Walter trying to get away and Ernest holding onto his arm.

"Poor Ernest," Iris said. "I bet he wishes he'd never got involved with this end of the business. He should just stick with growing the wheat."

"I'm afraid we've lost Ernest, honey. Once you've seen the lights of show biz, its hard to go back to the farm. Ernest is a bread-baking star in his own right."

Iris's eyes twinkled with mischief. "Bright lights, show biz, hard to go back to the farm. It sounds like you know this story from experience, Mom."

"Look who's talking, Miss My-boyfriend-is-Stuart-Watts. I don't see you suggesting we move back to Kansas."

Iris jumped up on the back of the truck with graceful ease. She held out her hand to her mother. "No, its fun to visit, but I wouldn't want to live here."

Bierocks

For the dough
2 cups warm water
2 packages dry yeast
¼ cup sugar
1 ½ tsp. kosher salt
8 T. butter, melted, plus 3 T. to finish the buns
1 egg
6–7 cups bread flour

For the filling
1 yellow onion, peeled and diced
1 ½ lbs. ground beef
2 cups red cabbage, shredded
2 cups green cabbage, shredded
Salt and pepper, hot sauce
Options: 1 cup yellow cheese, grated; ½ cup hard cheese, such as Parmesan or Romano, grated; 2 T. tomato paste; 1 cup diced cooked potatoes; 1 cup cooked rice.

Dissolve yeast in ½ cup warm water. When the yeast bubbles, about 5 minutes, add butter, egg, sugar, and salt. Add flour and knead with a bread hook or by hand, approximately 5 minutes. The dough should be elastic. Place in an oiled bowl, cover with a dish towel or clear film, and set aside until the dough has doubled, about 1 hour. Punch down and let rise again, about 30 minutes. You can chill the dough at this time and resume the process later.

In a heavy, large sauté pan that has been heated, brown the beef and onion together, adding a tablespoon of canola oil if the beef is too lean. Add cabbage after beef is brown and cover for 10 or 15 minutes over medium heat. Add salt, pepper, and a few drops of Tabasco or other hot sauce. Add cheese, rice or any of the options. Set aside to cool.

When the dough has completed its second rising, turn out on a floured surface and roll into thin sheets. Cut into 5-inch squares. Place 2 T. of the meat mixture in each square, fold over and pinch edges together so that there is a smooth side and the side with the seam. Place seam side down on an oiled baking sheet and let rise 20 minutes. Bake at 350 degrees for 15–20 minutes. Brush with melted butter when they come out of the oven and serve.

Six

General Irwin Mills marched up and down the inspection line. The entire staff of the Milling and Grain International Studies Laboratory was at attention, getting the last word from their boss before the celebrity bakers showed up.

"Name, rank, and serial number, and that is all you tell them, do you understand? We have to treat this as an enemy movement behind our own lines. I will be the one to give out information. I want everyone else to stay busy and productive. This interference is made necessary by the need for funds, so our work can go forward," the general said sternly. "BIG BREAD has the ill-founded notion that these people can be of use to us some day. I've tried to tell them we go straight to the enlisted man with our program. Who needs the junior officers?"

Several of the lab employees were shifting uncomfortably. They were used to the general using his military terms, but this time he seemed to really believe they were on some kind of military maneuvers, instead of simply having a bunch of bakers out for a tour.

The general checked his watch. "Everyone, let's all be together on this, down to the second. It's twelve hundred hours, thirty-two minutes, seventeen seconds. Everyone goes for a thirty-minute lunch at twelve forty-five. You will then have forty-five minutes to get your areas in shipshape. The tour is due to be here at two."

Every square inch of the lab was already shipshape but no one said a word. The general hadn't been himself all day. He seemed to be coming down with a cold or the flu but whenever anyone asked him if he felt all right, the general bit their head off. When the first person broke the inspection line and started to walk away, the general bellowed.

"I haven't said dismissed, have I troops?"

Several people spoke up quickly. "No, sir. Sorry, sir," and pulled the poor employee back into the line.

"Remember, this is the enemy. Be careful what you say. Now, troops, dismissed. Carry on."

As the lab employees bolted for the door, the general stood rigidly at attention, watching them each cross in front of him to get away. Then, as the last one left the room, he spun around and pointed his finger accusingly in the air. "You told me you would let me know who the traitor was. We were married thirty-five years. The least you could do is help me find the traitor!" he shouted to the empty room.

Heaven looked around. "This is nice," she said contentedly. They had moved ten miles north to Ernest Powell's farm, where the crowd had been subdued by a big farm lunch. It had been billed on the conference program as a Mennonite lunch and, after Walter's speech about the Mennonites being the root of all evil, the group was titillated to be surrounded by the descendants of the ones who brought 'Red Turkey' wheat to Kansas. And Ernest and the other Mennonite farmers and their families hadn't disappointed, not that anything racy happened, but the lunch was great.

The farm families had long tables set under big shade trees in the yard. There were vintage feed sack tablecloths draped handkerchief style over the tables and real china plates painted with faded roses and bluebirds. Ernest told them they always ate out here in the yard during wheat harvest, just like Kansas farmers had for a hundred years.

The crowd loved that, being part of wheat history and all. They had started taking photos at GRIP but now they really went into high gear snapping off shots, what with the quaint costumes that the Mennonites wore. From what Heaven could overhear, almost every baker here had a freelance assignment to do a story on the conference for a food magazine or the food section of his or her local paper. No time was being wasted.

The meal included exotic specialties like bierocks, a meat-filled turnover, and cherry moos, a sour cherry soup. There was also a delicious beef and cabbage borscht. Bread, of course, was well represented with loaves of Swedish-style rye, cinnamon-raisin, whole wheat-oatmeal, and dinner rolls called zwieback made of a soft buttery dough.

Pauline was having her third roll with lots of butter and apple butter. "I thought zwieback meant twice baked. I've only known it to be that hard toast you give babies when they're teething," Pauline said with her mouth full.

"Actually, there is another usage that refers to the double-bun structure of the roll, the smaller roll on the back of the larger roll, as in this case," Dieter explained as he dug in to his second bowl of borscht. They hadn't been able to shake him since the GRIP tour. Heaven was getting used to his authoritative ways. It was great to let someone else be in charge for a change.

"Dieter, you're a wealth of information," Heaven said with only mild sarcasm. "And what about these beer rocks?"

Dieter laughed indulgently. "B-I-E-R-O-C-K-S," he spelled. "I asked Ernest, and he said they dated from the 1700s, not these particular bierocks that we were served but the recipe for the dish." There was that appalling lack of a sense of humor again, Heaven thought. He had made it impossible for her to crack a joke about 200-year-old beer rocks.

Dieter, blissfully ignorant of his own stuffiness, continued. "I've been a baker since I was eight years old. This is enough time to be interested about the history of the craft," Dieter said as he pushed the borscht away. "You can tell these Mennonites spent some time in Germany on their way to the promised land. They are good with cabbage."

Heaven didn't even consider mentioning to Dieter that Russians cooked cabbage too, but she seemed to remember from her Kansas history course in junior high that the Mennonites had been kicked out of Germany before they went to Russia. No wonder the cabbage was up to Dieter's high standards.

Ernest Powell suddenly appeared up at the head of the table. "Excuse me ladies and gentlemen. I know our short lunch period is over and the general will be expecting us in Manhattan very soon. I just wanted you to know that, despite Mr. Jinks' doomsday report, we whose ancestors brought 'Red Turkey' wheat to this country are mighty glad they did."

There was applause from everyone. Ernest had taken it like a man before, and now it was his turn to dish a little back to Walter Jinks. "That does not mean I take lightly the sincere efforts on the behalf of mankind that Mr. Jinks has put forth. But there is room for more than one point of view in America. I'm sure you will all agree with me on that." Heads nodded in the affirmative.

"Now, he's got 'em where he wants 'em," Heaven whispered to Iris.

"And so now, I would ask this distinguished company to grant me a few short minutes to speak to you sometime during this conference about a matter that is very important to me, and one that is germane to the subject at hand—bread." Ernest looked around for someone with the authority to say yes. Program committee members huddled.

But Dieter couldn't wait for the ARTOS hierarchy to respond. He got up and clapped his hands for attention. "I know that no one who just enjoyed this delicious lunch would dream of refusing your polite request, Herr Powell. If nothing else, I will share some of my own time with you. I'm looking forward to what you have to say." With that he strode down to the end of the table and slapped Ernest on the shoulder, as if they were both members of the same lodge back home in Düsseldorf. The committee members fluttered over to the two men, clipboards poised to work Ernest into the schedule.

"Gosh, I wonder what Ernest is going to talk about. Maybe he's made some great new wheat-farming break-through," Pauline gushed as they walked toward the buses.

Heaven looked at Iris and shook her head slightly, trying to indicate to Iris that she shouldn't mention the bread machines. Heaven didn't want to spoil Ernest's moment, and she knew if Pauline were privy to the real topic of his interest, he would be the laughing stock of these baking snobs by the end of the day. Iris gave her mother a little conspiratorial grin and kept quiet.

Pauline turned to Iris. "Do you want to come on the bus with me? There were a few empty seats. I bet Dieter will sit near us."

Iris turned to her mother. Heaven gave her a thumbs up. "Go on, honey. We only have fifteen miles to go. I won't get too lonesome in that time. But you ride back to Kansas City with me later, OK? It'll be our last ride together before you leave."

"Oh, brother, how corny. Of course I wouldn't miss the trip home together. I learned things about you on the way here that you never spilled before." Iris touched her mother's arm and walked off with Pauline, and soon they were joined by their new best friend. Dieter Bishop walked toward the bus with his arms around both Pauline and Iris. "They look cute together," she murmured to no one in particular. You know its bad, when as a mother, a dictatorial German baker looks like a better match for your daughter than an English rock 'n' roller.

Heaven went over to Ernest's wife. She had seen him kiss her on the cheek and thought she could assume it was his wife, this being a religious community and all. "Mrs. Powell, I'm Heaven Lee. My brother is Del O'Malley. I really enjoyed the lunch and wondered if I might get the recipe for the bierocks from you."

Mrs. Powell didn't look as amused about Heaven's name as her husband had been but she smiled politely. "Let's go in the house and you can talk to Sara Akers. She is the best bierock baker in the county. Lord knows, she could use a little compliment right now, something to cheer her up. Not that anything will ever be able to—oh—I'm sorry, you probably don't know what happened. Our neighbors, the Akers, their son Ben was as nice a young man as you would ever want to find. He went to church without a whimper, made good grades in school, had a part-time job at the Farmer's Co-op to help the family."

Heaven nodded sympathetically. "I heard my brother and your husband mention the accident last night, when Mr. Powell came to borrow some tables. Did Ben's car get stranded on a train track?"

Betsy Powell shook her head, her eyes filling with tears at the remembering. "At least that would make some sense of this horrible tragedy. He, well, it seems he ran into the train, or laid down on the tracks or something. His car was a mile away, out on their property by a river that the kids always like to swim in."

"So, a suicide?" Heaven asked as they went up the stairs to the kitchen door.

Betsy clutched Heaven's arm. "Heavens, *no*," she almost yelled, with confusion showing on her face when she realized she'd used the word heaven to Heaven. Heaven realized that suicide was probably not acceptable as an explanation for these religious folks.

They paused at the door and Heaven tried to set Betsy Powell at ease. "I'm sorry I even mentioned it. You can be sure I won't say anything to make your neighbor feel worse than she already does."

The two women walked into a kitchen full of the murmurs of gentle feminine voices and the clanking of stacking dishes, with an occasional laugh punctuating the background noise. There were at least eight Mennonite ladies working on dish washing and clean-up, each in a prim, high-necked dress and bibbed apron, each with her hair tucked into a traditional net bonnet.

Even with these signs of the unique religion of this group, the scene reminded Heaven of many Sundays at her grandmother's house when she was a kid. A big meal in the middle of the day, after church of course, was the way Kansas families socialized. Sometimes an uncle or boy cousin would help clear the table, but back then the kitchen of a farm household was a female domain. Heaven loved hanging around the big girls, listening to all the gossip, which no one would ever think of as gossip but as news, even when she was small. She never took the option of going out to play with the other cousins. The kitchen was full of good smells and too much action to leave for some dumb game. Just like this one was now. Betsy Powell led her over to a big kitchen table. Two women were drying a mountain of silverware and placing it into piles to go back home with its owners.

Betsy went up to one of the women. "Sara, this is Del O'Malley's sister. She's here with this baking group and wants the recipe for your bierocks." Heaven noticed that Mrs. Powell didn't introduce her by name and she decided not to confuse the issue. Instead she sat down and pulled a small notebook and pen out of her bag. Then she smiled sweetly. Mrs. Powell seemed to decide it was all right to leave Heaven alone with her neighbor and moved to the area of the kitchen where the leftovers were being divided for everyone to take home.

"I must confess that even though I grew up here, I've never had bierocks until today," Heaven said as she pushed the pad and pen over towards the other woman. "They're delicious."

Sara Akers smiled wanly, then broke into tears silently. Heaven looked quickly around, not wanting Betsy Powell to catch this and think Heaven had made the grieving mother cry. Everyone was busy and the second silverware woman had gone over to the sink.

Heaven covered the trembling hands of the weeping woman with her own and patted, then withdrew her hands, not wanting to appear too forward. She really wanted to hug her and make the hurt go away but she knew that was impossible. "Ben loved my bierocks. He would eat them six at a time. I can't believe I'm never going to get to make them for him again," Sara Akers said quietly, wiping her eyes with a linen hankie.

Heaven could certainly speak honestly to this sad lady. "I have a daughter and I know it's every parent's worst fear. Everyone speaks so highly of your son."

Sara nodded. "Yes, he was a good boy, well adjusted and well liked. And you're right about it being every parent's nightmare. A child shouldn't die before his folks. And not knowing why or how this happened is something I don't think I can live with for the rest of my life."

"I know from my own childhood that the trains go pretty fast through this part of the country. Do you think he was walking along the tracks and it kinda snuck up on him?" asked Heaven.

Sara shook her head. "Why would he do a thing like that? If I didn't know better, I would think that someone did this to him but Ben didn't have an enemy in the world. It just makes no sense."

"You mean that someone could have knocked him out or drugged him and put him there to die?" Heaven asked bluntly. Those questions sounded awful out loud but clearly this mother was searching for answers that weren't necessarily going to sound pretty.

"Ben did not take drugs or drink alcohol. I think he may have had a beer once, but he told his father about it and promised it wouldn't happen again. If he was crazy enough to be on that track that night, it wasn't because of something he did consciously, I know that as sure as I know anything," Sara Akers said as she took the pen in her hand and stared down at the paper.

Heaven wanted to ask about an autopsy, but she was afraid it would cause a new round of tears. The body couldn't have been in very good shape after a run-in with a freight train. She switched the topic of conversation to food instead, babbling on about Cafe Heaven while Sara Akers wrote out her bierocks recipe.

Ernest Powell watched the two women from outside the kitchen windows. He was sure Del's sister was a good person, after all Del was the salt of the earth. But anyone who went by a stage name couldn't have much to talk to his wife and Sara Akers about. He would be glad when all these high falutin' cooks went back to where they belonged.

General Irwin Mills was trapped by his mind in the bathroom stall. What's more, the walls of the stall were moving, coming nearer, then farther in undulating rhythms. The general was crouched in the corner, wedged in between the toilet and the wall. Sweat was pouring down his face. Hearing someone come in, he stepped quietly up on the seat of the stool, bending down so neither his feet nor his head could be seen. The someone used the urinal and left. The general rushed to the men's room door, throwing the bolt in place so no one else could come in. Immediately, someone tried to pull the door open and the general, crawling on all fours, took cover under the row of sinks. He sat there for five minutes or so. One of the sinks was dripping; other than that, it was quiet. The general got to his feet and looked in the mirror.

"You sissy. Don't let them see you like this. Get a grip, man," he lectured himself sternly. The full salute to his image. "Carry on."

He filled a basin with cold water and sank his face in it. It was most amazing. He was sure he could breathe under water.

Heaven looked up and down the halls. The Milling and Grain International Studies Laboratory certainly had better funding than GRIP, she thought as she glanced into the well-appointed test kitchens. The place seemed to be run like a well-oiled machine. Workers in hazmet-style jumpsuits were going about their business silently. In one room, two men were spraying what looked to be cheese dust in a rotating round metal drum filled with what looked to be corn chips. Two women were working behind a glass door marked Experimental Kitchen #4. Heaven couldn't resist. She detoured in.

"What happens in here?" Heaven asked.

The two women looked startled, as if they weren't used to visitors.

"The conference is down the hall," one of them stammered.

"Oh, I know. I'm on my way there, but you two looked interesting. What are you working on?" Heaven asked, now relishing the challenge of getting some information from the women.

They exchanged looks, obviously weighing the trouble they might get into by giving out any info against getting this intruder out of their domain. "We're trying to develop a fat-free doughnut," the spokeswoman for the duo said.

"Neat," Heaven said. "So you're going to bake it?"

"Oh, no. It has to be fried. A doughnut's not a doughnut unless its fried, the general says. Plus the sweet cake company that's paying us insists on it," the other one piped in.

Heaven made for the door. "Lots of luck. Sounds like you have your work cut out for you." She continued down the corridor. They must love it when companies ask for stupid stuff like that. They could be working on an impossible project like that for years. Either that or they'll have to use Olestra, she thought with a shudder. Of course, this place probably invented Olestra or helped invent it, she realized as she walked past another fully equipped lab.

Heaven rounded a corner and looked into a large amphitheater-style class room. The lecture had already started so she slipped into the back of the room and stood. General Irwin Mills was holding forth, eyes bright, his white lab coat starched to the it-could-stand-alone state. He had written his name and the name of the lab in block letters on the blackboard. It reminded Heaven of college. Anyone not signed up for Grains 101 please leave the building.

The general was sweating profusely, beads of water turning into trickles running down his face and head. Heaven wondered if he was nervous about having all the bigwig bakers here. He certainly had his speech prepared. "Of course we know that bread has the deepest penetration into people's homes of any other food category. Seventy-five percent of women shoppers are employed and ninety percent of those feel pressed for time. That's where the manufactured bread segment of grain-based foods comes in. Those women aren't going to bake their own bread, no they are not," the general exclaimed in a way that defied argument. "Forty-three percent of all bread is consumed as in-home sandwiches, twenty-two percent as toast, and sixteen percent as plain bread. That leaves eighteen percent for you, at least those of you who are affiliated with restaurants. That eighteen percent of bread that is consumed in restaurants is up three percent, making inroads against in-home consumption. By the way, fifteen percent of the American public ate a bagel last year, a rise of ten percent in the last five years." The general said the word bagel as if it were part of a commie pinko plot. The fountain of bread statistics continued flowing.

"Last year the per capita flour consumption reached 149 pounds, up from the disgraceful performance of 1970 when it hit a historic low of 110 pounds," he snarled, as if the bakers in the room had been personally responsible for the lack of interest in bread in the 70s. Then he pulled an easel out from the wall and stood erect and unsmiling next to it.

"You have probably heard of our work with hard white winter wheat, a grain that makes whole wheat flour bread that looks like bleached flour bread," the general said proudly. "In the last three months," the general intoned, wiping his forehead with a starched handkerchief, "we have had a major breakthrough here at the lab, one that the public is probably not aware of yet." Now he had let everyone in the room know that he considered them part of the unwashed masses known as the public, not as the insiders they assumed they were. He lifted the cover on the easel and showed a display of food product boxes with the BIG BREAD logo. Then he pointed in the middle of the crowd. "We've been working together with a team from BIG

BREAD in Kansas City. Mr. Patrick Sullivan is here today representing that research team. BIG BREAD assisted financially in the white wheat project." An embarrassed looking young man stood briefly and sat quickly down. Heaven figured that white wheat gave BIG BREAD a chance to trick kids into eating something a little better for them.

The general forced a stiff smile. Heaven thought he must be getting the flu because now he was shaking as if he had the chills. "As some of you may know," he sniffed and you could tell he was sure none of them knew, "we have worked with BIG BREAD in establishing a bio-genetics department here at International Studies. BIG BREAD has been very generous in their financial support. That department's first research has been in the development of gene-modified wheat. This work has proven successful in creating plants more efficient in accepting various herbicides and insecticides while increasing their yield at the same time."

Now the murmurs in the crowd that had started with the white wheat announcement reached a low roar. People were saying, "Oh no," out loud. The general was undeterred. These pantywaist wimps might flinch at the words insecticide and herbicide but the general did not.

"I know that you started your day at the GRIP research facility not far from here so I am sure you will understand the implications of this next announcement. Our latest joint venture with BIG BREAD has produced a wheat clone that will produce year after year. A perennial wheat plant that will eliminate the necessity for retraining the world's population to eat native grasses like animals as Mr. Jinks would have them do."

"No, No!"

Heaven was startled by the intensity of those "Nos" coming from right next to her. They penetrated the hubbub the entire room was in. It was Walter Jinks himself, who must have slipped in the room after Heaven had. He was rushing down to the general with blood in his eyes, his hands outstretched as if to strangle the other man.

Before the agitated scientist could make it to the lectern level of the room to do bodily harm, he was grabbed, by Ernest Powell, who had been sitting in the front row again. The general was red-faced, but seemed to be enjoying this confrontation. In fact, he seemed to be having the time of his life.

"I remember you. Jinks. During 'Nam, you came to Ft. Riley and disrupted the main highway with a sit-in. I was unable to get my food supplies for two days because of you and your mangy crew. I recommended running you all down with an APC at the time," the general shouted as Ernest and two others tried to restrain Walter. Heaven remembered from growing up near Ft. Riley that APC stood for armored personnel carrier.

"You can't do this, Mills." Walter screeched. "You'll poison the planet. You must be stopped."

As Walter was being escorted out of the room, the general, who looked like he would love nothing better than to go out behind the building and have a fist fight with the distraught man, straightened his tie and once more addressed the group. "I'm afraid that that's all I can tell you at this time about our amazing new wheat clone. Just know that you were here when history was made. The concluding part of the program today will be held outside. Because we store our own grain here at the lab, we thought it would be educational for you to see the entire process of what happens after the grain is harvested. Even though it is not harvest time, we have transported a truckload of wheat from one of our satellite facilities. We'll imagine it just came from the field. We will demonstrate what happens to it from the time it comes to the grain elevator, through the milling process. Please follow me to the back of the building, where our storage silos are located."

The general marched out of the room, leaving a chaotic scene behind. Heaven looked for Iris and Pauline, who were waving at her as they made their way up the stairs to the exit. As she watched them someone tapped her on the shoulder. She jumped, edgy from all the confrontation.

"I just wanted to introduce myself. I'm Patrick Sullivan. I recently was transferred to Kansas City and your restaurant is one of the things that keeps me sane."

It was the young man that had been introduced as a BIG BREAD bigwig. "Hi, Patrick. It's that bad for you in Kansas City, is it, not that I don't appreciate the compliment. Are you participating in this conference or did you just come out here so we could have a hate target?" Heaven asked as they stepped out in the hall. Patrick looked like he wanted to walk with her but she was still waiting for the girls.

He paused, unsure of what to do. "Oh, no. I'm a member of this group, and I'm in for the duration. We're even going to have ARTOS tour BIG BREAD as a gesture of friendship. It's funny, even with my Catholic background, I never really understood the role of the sacrificial lamb until now."

Heaven couldn't help but smile. "At least you have a sense of humor about it. And you can't be surprised you're not the most popular guy at this particular party. After all, your company isn't exactly part of this artisan bread movement."

Patrick pushed his wire-rimmed glasses up on his nose, something he did when he was nervous. "Someone had to do it, they said. I just wish . . . Well, I'm glad to meet you. I hope you'll come to the tour on Saturday." Just as he was getting ready to follow the crowd out of the building, Pauline and Iris arrived on the scene and Heaven could see him hesitate. But she ignored him. They had dirt to dish and they certainly couldn't have him hanging around when they did it. He got the idea quickly that she wasn't going to introduce him and went away.

"Poor Mr. Jinks," Pauline wailed. "His whole career, years of work down the drain if General Mills has anything to do with it."

Heaven slipped her arms through both of the young women's arms and the three of them followed the crowd. "I wouldn't deal Walter Jinks out of the game, yet. He probably knows more about perennial wheat than the whole company of BIG BREAD and everyone here at this creepy International Studies Laboratory put together."

Iris was shaking her head. "If I tried to tell my friends at Oxford about this, they wouldn't believe me, they'd think it was the plot of my next short story or something. Who knew a simple thing like wheat, or bread for that matter, could produce such passion?"

Heaven laughed. "Yeah, this is important stuff your Mom is involved in. I hope we can make it through the next hour without Walter punching the general or Ernest punching Walter. Everyone is so serious and sure they are the only one with the correct position. It does tickle me to see all these celebrity bakers be completely upstaged by a bunch of wheat farmers and scientists though. No one has been able to throw attitude around or have a diva fit. You have to take a number for that in this group."

Pauline nodded. "It's like they're stunned and thrilled to be in the middle of it, all at the same time, sort of like being in New York the week of the James Beard Awards. Of course, I've never actually been to the James Beard Awards, but I can just imagine what it would be like, and I've read about it in *Food Arts* magazine."

For the purposes of the outdoor demonstration, General Mills had a wireless microphone. He had given the group exactly seven minutes to troop out to the grain-elevator area, then had started his speech. Heaven walked slowly around the crowd, letting her mind wander, not paying that much attention to what he was saying. She had seen wheat coming off a truck many times before, falling down between grates in the unloading area. Two men were standing by the scoop truck, hazmet suits on and breathing masks in place over their noses and mouth. The general was explaining how dangerous grain dust was, pointing to the masks on the workers.

When the last bushels of wheat kernels had been scooped out of the truck bed, one of the men got in the truck and drove it away from the elevator. The general went over to the elevator motor and turned it on, pointing to the top of the elevator where a waterfall of grain began falling from the chute into the silo. The motor he activated was pumping the wheat that had been dumped in the holding bin below the ground up on a conveyer belt covered with a round metal duct to protect it from inclement weather. Heaven could see this was a real crowd-pleaser. People were oohhing and aahhing and taking lots of photos.

The general looked sternly at his audience, mopping his brow. He had been pretty agitated since the run-in with Walter. "Even with this round design of the storage unit, the silo, grain storage is very dangerous. Spontaneous combustion occurs an average of twenty-seven times per year in America resulting in five deaths and the loss of $120 million worth of product, because once these fires start, they are very difficult to put out and are usually allowed to burn themselves out. Eleven deaths a year occur from suffocation of elevator workers who accidentally fall into storage units," the general explained in a way that let everyone know he had no sympathy for these poor hapless workers who must not have been following safety procedures. The general was very good at intonation.

Now he picked up a five-gallon plastic pail. "So we can follow this same wheat through the process, I will go up to the top of the storage unit and get us a sampling, which we will put through a very simple series of tests before we take it into our milling facility, the same tests for water content and purity that grain would be tested for at any storage facility in the country." The general gave the microphone to one of his aides and hopped on a tiny metal platform on the outside of the silo. It was similar to the lifts that run on construction sites, but it didn't have a cage around it, just wire fence material with a hinged gate that came up to about the knee. You just stepped on, turned it on, and up you went. The general seemed to be gliding up the side of the grain elevator on his own steam, like an angel or one of those levitating yogis in India. Heaven had to hand it to him. He had taken the mundane workings of every Kansas grain elevator and turned it into quite a show. The visiting bakers were enthralled, clicking photos again.

Then it happened.

General Mills, who had been looking down at the crowd with absolutely no expression one way or the other, reached the top of the elevator. The lift stopped. Instead of holding his pail over the rush of grain being fed into the top of the silo, he dropped the bucket, straightened his tie, pointed in the air as though to indicate something, opened the wire gate on the lift, and jumped. Jumped wasn't really the word for it, because that implies an energetic movement. He just stepped into space, tumbling down with the same ease he had gone up, just a lot faster.

There was a moment frozen in time when the crowd couldn't believe their eyes. Then there was a collective gasp, an intake of breath. It took those few seconds for people to accept the fact they had just seen a man fly to his probable death. The whole crowd then leapt into action, talking and running around like a bunch of chickens with their heads cut off.

Heaven looked for Iris first, wanting to shield her daughter from this ugly reality. Iris and Pauline were standing with their hands covering their eyes. They looked like small girls do when the scary part of the movie comes on the screen. Heaven headed for them, deep in the crowd.

One of the general's staff members ran over to the control panel on the side of the elevator and, in a panic, tried to shut off the grain pumping above. Instead, the chute swung wildly and rotated to the outside of the silo, the deluge of wheat now coming down on the prone body of General Mills.

"Call 911," several people yelled. One of the hazmet boys ran toward the door to the lab. Heaven looked up just in time to see Patrick Sullivan calmly turn off the grain elevator engine, and with it, the waterfall of wheat.

Iris looked up at her mother and hugged her. "Mom, are you OK? What happened? The platform must have given way or something," she said. "Do you think he's . . ."

Heaven nodded. "That silo looks like its about forty or fifty feet tall. Maybe he could survive if he fell in water, or even tall grass. But it looks like he landed right on the concrete and partially on the beginning of the metal grate. I'm afraid he's dead."

Dieter Bishop was directing a team of men who were uncovering the general's body. They were coughing and choking and the air was full of grain dust.

Heaven couldn't help herself. "Stay right here," she ordered the two young women. She made a beeline for the side of the elevator where she had just seen Patrick Sullivan. He wasn't there. Heaven looked around for Ernest Powell and Walter Jinks but couldn't spot them either. She shaded her eyes and tried to look straight up into the sun at the one-man lift. As far as she could see no parts were dangling and nothing obviously broken was sticking out. It was hard to imagine anything breaking around the general. Heaven had a feeling he had been a maintenance freak from the spotless look of the place.

She walked over to Dieter, who stood up from kneeling over the prone body. He was coughing and wiping his face, now grimy from the dust.

"Try CPR," someone yelled.

Dieter shook his head. "It won't help. He's gone."

And so he was. Heaven shoved her way to the front of the macabre circle. Every part of the general's body was going in a different direction. He looked like a puppet that someone had dropped in a heap. Luckily his eyes were closed and only one side of his face was showing, as though he had fallen asleep on the pavement. Heaven saw something that she didn't quite understand. She leaned down for a closer look. The tip of the general's tongue was hanging out of his mouth and it was black.

Cherry Moos

Cherry seeds are another thing the Mennonites brought with them from Russia to Kansas. One of the Old World recipes they continued to make was a cold dessert soup from the fruits of these imported trees. Again, this is a hybrid recipe, a little Mennonite, a little Russian—although the Mennonites wouldn't approve of the wine.

2 pounds fresh cherries
½ cup sugar
2 cups rosé wine
1 cup orange juice
2 cinnamon sticks
1 bay leaf
2 cloves
2 cardamom seeds
2 T. lemon juice
1 cup sour cream or crème fraîche if available

Pit the cherries and reserve 1 cup. Combine the rest of the cherries in a medium sauce pan with the sugar, wine, orange juice, and seasonings. Simmer until the cherries are very soft, 20–30 minutes. Strain out the spices and puree the mixture in a food processor. Return to the sauce pan and add the reserved cherries and simmer for five minutes. Cool and add the sour cream and lemon juice. Chill and serve.

Seven

"What happened next?" The question was directed toward Pauline. It was eight-thirty Friday morning and a powwow that normally would take place at Sal's was convened in the kitchen of Cafe Heaven so Pauline could participate and make bread at the same time.

Mona Kirk would give Sal a blow-by-blow later as he always had early customers and couldn't get away from the barber shop. Heaven had called the restaurant the night before and told Murray and Joe and Chris to show up bright and early.

Heaven and Iris had stopped for bagels on the way to work. Iris had agreed to come and do prep work so both her mother and Pauline could go to the conference. She wasn't a cook but she could follow instructions and a prep list.

"Then we came home," Pauline said. She looked around the table at the disappointment on the eager faces and decided she needed to add a little more detail. She was a novice at these crime-scene descriptions. "I mean hours later after the medical emergency team had been there and the police and the coroner and all that."

"Did they question you?" Mona asked as she inhaled a Black Russian bagel piled with cream cheese. Crime made Mona hungry.

"They took everyone's name and address and asked each person for their version of what they'd seen. I told them I was staring at Walter Jinks and didn't even see the actual fall," Pauline explained.

"And Mom thinks that's important," Iris added.

The three women had told the story like a rotating Greek chorus. Murray had tried to organize the material, writing down the cast of characters on a legal pad. Now he started looking through his notes. "Let's see, I'll find Walter Jinks. He's the . . ."

"Former peacenik, experimental farm, perennial polycultures. The police were going to question Walter further," Chris said like the kid who always had the answers in math class. Chris hadn't tried to write and listen at the same time.

"And," Heaven threw in with high drama in her voice, "the one who had to be escorted from the building when the general dropped his big announcement. Walter said the general had to be stopped in front of all of us!"

Joe held up his hand. "I know, I know. The general stole Walter's thunder by doing perennial wheat instead of diversifying the way Walter thinks the world should do."

"Very good, Joe," Heaven said as she helped Pauline shape some dough into loaves. Pauline was keeping a nervous eye on Heaven's loaf formation.

"Of course Mother isn't sure the general has any perennial wheat. She thinks the general just said that to get Walter's goat," Iris said.

"The general doesn't have anything now, that's for sure," Murray said. "Did the police say anything about it being, you know, foul play?"

Heaven shook her head. "Well, someone ratted out Walter right away, and they did ask him to come down to the station. But I don't think there was enough time for Walter to rig an accident between their argument and the general's fall. Walter would have had to know in advance what the general was going to say, pretend to be surprised, and rig the elevator between lunch and the general's announcement. And how would Walter know that the general would be going up the elevator vis-à-vis the demonstration, even if he was crazy enough and angry enough to kill him? I asked the investigating officer if it was possible that the general committed suicide. 'Highly unlikely' was all the Manhattan detective would say."

"So this Walter Jinks pitches a fit and says 'you must be stopped' to the general and gets thrown out and then you all go outside and the general takes a swan dive off a silo. Pauline, you just happen to be staring at this Jinks character right at the moment of impact, not his of course," Mona said as she paced around the kitchen. "This could be big, Pauline. How'd he look? Did he have a little gadget he was fiddling with, a timer or something?"

Pauline looked down. "Well, I don't really know. I didn't look at his hands, or at least I don't remember his hands. I was just thinking about how sorry I felt for him and I didn't even think it was strange that he had hung around after the argument. I guess I'd gotten used to his being around all day. But if he'd been doing anything really weird, I think I would have noticed. But you know how it is when you're day dreaming and then someone startles you? All you remember is what startled you. Suddenly Iris grabbed my arm and made this funny noise and I looked up for the general and well, he was on the ground. I didn't think about Mr. Jinks again until the police asked me for my version of the, ah, accident."

Mona didn't let Pauline's sketchy and vague descriptions daunt her. "This is like one of those locked-room murders, you know? Where no one could get in or out yet the victim turns up with a dagger in his back. A hundred people were watching one man go up the side of a grain elevator. No one else was near him and he falls to his death, and yet it doesn't seem like an accident. I love it, don't you, Heaven?"

Heaven nodded her head toward Mona as she worked. "It's like an outdoor locked-door mystery. If you could have seen the look on his face you'd know why this is so puzzling. It wasn't a look of oh, my God, I slipped, or oh my God, the lift broke. It was very strange. I can hardly wait to compare notes with some of the ARTOS folks. There was no chance yesterday because the police asked us not to talk to each other while we waited to give our statements, and then everyone left as soon as possible.

"I really wanted Pauline to ride back on the bus and try to listen to what the bakers had to say about the accident," Heaven explained. "But Pauline said she wasn't good at eavesdropping and excitement always made her sleepy." Heaven's eyebrows shot up but she stopped herself from calling Pauline a wimp. "She said she'd just fall asleep as soon as the bus started moving and so I let her come with Iris and me in the van. And sure enough, they both fell asleep."

"I'm not ashamed. Hanging with Mom is too much for me. There's never a dull moment. Even in supposedly bucolic Kansas, we turn up in the middle of a police investigation," Iris murmured with a bagel in her mouth. Pauline said nothing but looked apologetic for being such a light-weight on the investigative team.

Joe glanced at both of the young women with an expression that said "what sorry excuses for amateur detectives you two are." Joe and Chris had helped with several little problems at Cafe Heaven and they imagined themselves just one step from opening a private investigating agency. "Heaven, what do we do next? Do you really think it was a fluke accident?"

Heaven looked at her watch and then reluctantly at the assembled group. She had flashed on the general's black tongue while they were going through the events of yesterday. Should she tell everyone now and ask someone to . . . no. She wanted to do the research herself. She slipped off her apron and washed her hands as she talked. "Next, Pauline and I have to be at the Board of Trade by ten. This conference is still going on. A fatal so-called accident won't stop the bakers. After all, the general wasn't a member of ARTOS and really wasn't even very nice to us. And he was doing terrible things with this evil biogenetic research. If we weren't booked every minute of this weekend and if it wasn't Iris's last weekend in town, I might go back out there and poke around.

"I will say this, the general didn't seem like the type to A. kill himself, B. let the equipment fall into disrepair, or C. make a silly mistake and step off into space. But since I don't have the time we are just going to have to let the authorities do their jobs."

The room was quiet. They couldn't believe Heaven had just said what she said. Heaven always wanted to explore what was around the next corner, authorities be damned, and the staff expected to be part of that. This time she seemed oblivious to all the possibilities for interference.

"Murray, your stuff is on the bar in the same manila envelope you left it in. I made comments on all your articles with post-its and I marked the three I think you should send to New York. See you guys later."

The whole crew looked as if they had just had a big candy bar taken away. They were used to Heaven handing out assignments when they got in the middle of trouble. If Heaven didn't have time, that didn't necessarily stop everyone else, did it?

The Board of Trade was used to big groups visiting. They had a visitors' gallery over the trading floor and a visitor guide who gave a snappy lecture about what goes on in futures trading. According to the guide, the impetus behind commodities futures trading was to stabilize the price of wheat or any other commodity, such as corn, soybeans, minerals, or petroleum products. A futures contract was an agreement to take delivery of the commodity for a specific price at a specific future date. By buying an option on a futures contract, the traders offer the right to take possesion of wheat in, say, March of next year, without requiring the other traders to actually take posession of the wheat. Options provide protection against adverse price movements without eliminating the potential for profit.

The guide was pointing at various parts of the trading floor where grown men in brightly colored jackets were yelling and shouting at each other and waving their arms wildly. These were the futures traders engaged in the highest stress profession in Kansas City.

The ARTOS group, however, were less than high energy, subdued after the excitement of the day before. The Board of Trade was full of drama however, each transaction meant thousands and sometimes hundreds of thousands of dollars were trading hands. The air was charged with the same kind of excitement you felt when images of the New York Stock Exchange appeared on TV. As they got the idea of what was happening down below, the bakers were warming to the task at hand, asking lots of questions and making notes. Heaven spotted Dieter Bishop. He was standing by Pauline, holding forth, as usual. Heaven slid over, hoping to get a reading on what the out-of-towners thought about the accident.

Dieter turned to Heaven with a smile. "So this is how you maintain the price of your flour with some stability. Very interesting." Then Dieter was reminded of his own lofty position. "Of course, a lot of the bakers that are members of ARTOS use specialty mills or grind their own flours like I do. I even grow my own rye," he said proudly.

Heaven grinned. These artisan bakers sure didn't want to be mistook for a regular Joe. "Of course. This futures thing is just for the common run-of-the-mill user of flour, not boutique guys like you. There are not only futures contracts for wheat but futures for flour. Lots of large cereal companies and people like BIG BREAD contract months in advance for a price on their flour. It's called "forward flour buying." Sometimes they win and sometimes they lose at this because there isn't the option clause for "forward flour buying." The price can go down from what they've promised to pay, so they can hedge their potential losses here as well. It turns out that this whole world of grain-based foods is full of gamblers. It wasn't until yesterday that I knew how exciting it really was," Heaven said, trying to get the subject back to the accident.

Dieter appraised Heaven. "So, what do you think? Did Walter go out and jimmy the lift on the grain elevator?" he asked.

"Oh, Dieter, I don't know. There wasn't much time for that. How would Walter know, hours beforehand, that the general would announce some competing scheme that would make him angry enough to kill and that we were all trooping outside for Wheat 101, part two? How would he know the general was the one that would go up the lift? Some underling of the general's could have gone up after the grain. Couldn't it have just been an accident?"

"Anything is possible, Heaven, but the general reminded me of my grandfather. A place for everything and everything in its place, my grandfather used to say. He had official inspection tours of his own house, for Christ's sake, where he marched through the rooms with his housekeeper looking for a speck of dust or a chair out of place. Men like that rarely let equipment break down," Dieter said, echoing Heaven's own assessment of the situation.

Before Heaven could pump Dieter for any more theories, the trading floor broke into high-pitched pandemonium. The usual yelling had gone up several decibels. Heaven peered down at her friend, David Gibbs, who was right in the middle of all the flurry. All the floor clerks, the people who weren't brokers but assisted with the trading on the floor, were busy on the phones, talking to their counterparts on the floor of the Chicago Board of Trade. The brokers that took care of cash trading, the actual sale of wheat and soybeans and corn instead of futures contracts, had all gotten up from their desks and were watching the frenzy in the pit with interest. The Board of Trade tour guide went out in the hall and came back moments later, her eyes shining with excitement.

Heaven moved towards the guide, anxious to get the scoop. "What's going on down there?"

"BIG BREAD," she said breathily. "They've, they've applied for a patent for a genetically engineered wheat seed. Nobody has ever done that before."

"Why that's ridiculous, you can't patent food crops, something the whole world uses," Dieter Bishop said with his usual confidence.

Heaven shook her head. "I don't know Dieter. I read a newspaper article a few months ago about some scientist in Colorado patenting quinoa and I think she got away with it."

"The South American grain?"

"The very one. It's causing a big to-do at the United Nations. Are scientists robbing native peoples of ancient knowledge, will these scientists have a monopoly over our food supply, questions like that. I remembered the article yesterday when Walter and the general started talking about their perennials."

Dieter looked down on the trading floor and then at the baking guild members. "Scientists? Of course, it would not be the scientists who would ultimately have control. You know that, Heaven. It would be the food companies, people like BIG BREAD."

"And the whole world would eat white bread and like it," Heaven commented wryly.

There was an intense round of yelling from the trading floor, then a bell sounded. It was one-fifteen in the afternoon and business closed for the day with a bang.

Hot Hacked Chicken

1 large whole frying chicken
¼ cup sesame oil
½ cup Thai sweet chili sauce
1 cup sherry
¼ cup good-quality soy sauce, medium body
½ cup chunky peanut butter
¼ cup Rooster sauce, a chili and garlic sauce available at
    most Asian stores
¼ cup minced fresh ginger
Cilantro leaves and black sesame seeds for garnish

Rinse your chicken and pat it dry with paper towels. Put the bird in a shallow baking dish on a rack and start the roasting process. Bake for 30 minutes at 400 degrees. This will crisp up the skin so it won't stick to the foil in the next step.

Combine all the other ingredients in a bowl. Take the chicken out of the oven and baste with the sauce. Spoon about ¼ cup sauce in the cavity of the bird. Cover with foil and bake at 350 degrees for 40 minutes. Remove the bird and baste again. Bake another 20 minutes, basting often. Many of the ingredients have sugar in them so the bird will turn a dark brown. This is good, even a little black won't hurt a bit. Any sauce you have left over you should bring to a boil, simmer 5 minutes and serve with the chicken.

Now, how to hack: With a Chinese cleaver or large French knife cut across the bird in the middle. Then on each half, cut across again, near where the legs and wings meet the body. Separate the front and back of the bird, as well as the 2 legs and wings. Garnish with cilantro leaves and black sesame seeds.

Eight

Murray pulled up in the parking lot of the Milling and Grain International Studies Laboratory. He had never been in Manhattan, Kansas, before but it had been easy to find.

Murray left Cafe Heaven with every intention of going home. The next thing he knew he was on I-70, heading west. He remembered Pauline saying it took about two hours to get there, so after he sped through Topeka, he watched the names of the Kansas towns on the exit signs. Soon enough, a sign said Manhattan exit, two miles. Now that he was here in the pretty college town, he wasn't sure what he could accomplish. But he was tickled pink he had followed his hunch and hit the road.

Something had happened to Murray after he accepted the writing assignment from the *Times*. It was like his fairy godmother had waved her magic wand and, poof, he was an investigative reporter again. Today that meant he couldn't go home and forget about the strange story Heaven and Pauline and Iris had told. The circumstances around the death of the general pointed to a good story, and even if the general's fall wasn't murder, there were still lots of good angles that now seemed to be calling out to Murray.

The business of the genetically engineered crops was a potentially interesting story line. So was the annual wheat versus perennial wheat idea. Murray also wondered how much topsoil actually was lost in America each year. Did *New York Times* readers even care about topsoil? One thing Murray knew from his past experience was that, topsoil or no, *New York Times* readers did like to find out yet another way the world was going to hell in a handbasket. They'll love this, he thought, as he got out of the car.

Murray entered the building and went up to the receptionist. "Hi there, I'm Murray Steinblatz. I write for the *New York Times* and I have an appointment with General Mills."

The receptionist quivered all over. "You don't know?"

"Know what?" Murray asked innocently.

"The general, an accident yesterday. The general is, he would hate me telling you this, he was such a stickler for going through channels. Maybe I should call someone." The receptionist looked at Murray's innocent face. What could it hurt? "The general is dead," she proclaimed.

Murray looked alarmed. He looked surprised. He was a good actor. "Dead! How terrible! You're right, maybe you should call someone. I've come a long way. The general was going to show me the whole operation. This is just awful." Murray looked at the nameplate on the desk. "Diane, I bet you are all just sick about this. I'm surprised you're even open if this happened yesterday."

"Oh, the general would have wanted us to carry on. That was one of his favorite sayings, carry on. I'll call his assistant in the test kitchen. He didn't have a personal secretary. Said he didn't have a personal life so why would he need a personal secretary. Oh, dear, I'm babbling."

"No you're not, Diane. I would sure appreciate getting to talk to that assistant, maybe still getting to take the tour of the laboratory and the research you're doing here, since you are carrying on. I'll just read this milling magazine and let you get back to your work." Murray made a pretense of picking up a magazine off a small table that was between two chairs in the area. Before he sat down, of course, he acted like he had just remembered his manners. "Oh, by the way, what happened, a car accident?"

"Car accident? Oh, the general. Oh no, it was right out in back. Just a minute. I'll call the lab, then, well, it was just awful. There were all these fancy bakers here for a tour and it happened with everyone looking on. I've never been questioned by the police before. . . ."

"The police, you've got to be kidding," Murray broke in, wide eyed. He waited while she put in her call on his behalf.

"He says he didn't know anything about you coming, but that's no surprise; the general didn't always tell us everything. The general said information was on a need-to-know basis. So he'll be out in ten minutes."

Murray grinned like a Cheshire cat. "Thank you for interceding for me. Now tell me about the police. Say, do you by chance have any coffee around here, Diane? I'm buying."

Heaven swung into the parking lot of the Westport Library. She had not gone to lunch with the ARTOS group, opting to stop by the cafe and make sure everyone was present and accounted for. They had been slammed with guests for lunch so she had taken off her fancy black Italian leather jacket and put on her chef's coat. She slipped out of the high heels and put on her kitchen clogs, the ones she bought in Paris at the chef's-wear store. For an hour she worked the line, pushing grilled salmon with berry sauce and chicken crepes out to the dining room. Then she changed her outfit again and slipped out the back door.

She needed ten minutes at the library, then she would meet up with ARTOS at the next event, the sourdough workshop. Since Heaven really wanted to learn to make good sourdough, she certainly didn't want to be too late. It was one forty-five, the session started at two and she was shooting for being there by two-fifteen. She hurried inside the library.

By the time Heaven arrived at the kitchens of the Hearth and Home Bakery, the sourdough session had already started. One of the owners of Hearth and Home was a nationally recognized sourdough expert. The group was at rapt attention, with five or six bakers up front, ready to do hands-on demonstrations. Chairs were stuck everywhere around the big production room. Heaven found one and sat down. She could see Pauline and Dieter near the front.

"Sourdough is alive. It is a mass of fermenting yeast, flour, and water that leavens and flavors a larger dough," the speaker was explaining. "You make sourdough by combining water with organic whole grain flour and allowing the natural yeasts present in the air and the flour to grow and multiply over a period of time. Sourdough takes time and patience." The speaker turned and looked intently at the BIG BREAD representatives. "That's why those in the mass-production of bread have never jumped on the sourdough bandwagon. Yes, time is an ingredient, just as sugar, flour, and butter can be. Time gives us a culture of sour, tangy dough strong enough to raise a larger mass of dough."

Heaven found her mind wandering. She wanted to learn about sourdough, she really did. Her hand slipped into her bag and she pulled out the photocopied pages from the library. Now what would make a person's tongue turn black?

The speaker went over to a covered crock that one of the bakers pushed his way. He peeled back the film covering the top of the crock and a yeasty, sour aroma came from the opening. A murmur of recognition went through the crowd. "Sourdough is the oldest leavener known. What did mankind do before there were cute little packages of yeast at the grocery store? Communities used their own sourdough or ate unleavened bread. We artisan bakers know we could buy predictable yeasts through the commercial bread manufacturing channels, but we reject that method." This statement was followed by a look at the BIG BREAD forces who were starting to shift uncomfortably in their chairs. "The wine-making industry in California had their fling with these test tube yeasts that were supposed to bring consistency to their wines. But now, more and more wine makers have gone back to using only the natural wild yeasts in the air to ferment their wines and their customers like it. So it is in bread making, each one of us has a truly unique tasting sourdough bread because of the different spring waters and wild yeasts in our home areas. Even the air brings different organisms with it to the culture. And like the wine makers, we've found that customers appreciate the added flavor this natural process gives the bread."

Heaven, her attention divided, looked down at her papers. According to the reference book at the library, silver nitrate will turn the skin black. Heaven wasn't really sure that tongue skin would have the same rules as regular skin but you had to start somewhere. What was silver nitrate? Another reference book had revealed it to be an irritant compound, $AgNO_3$, that in contact with organic matter turns black. It's used in photography and in medicine as an antiseptic and caustic. As an amateur photographer, Heaven knew how strong those chemicals were. Had the general swallowed his developing fluid? Maybe he had burned his tongue on something and had used silver nitrate; no, Heaven stopped herself, that made no sense. You didn't put some nasty tasting chemical compound on your tongue for a burn. In fact, you usually did nothing for a tongue burn, she realized. You usually just let it be sore for a day or two until it was better.

"We have started the process of making sourdough by making a chef. A chef is a piece of aged dough that has captured wild yeasts. To make this chef is a four-day process, and we have an example of the chef as it looks each day here on the counter for you to examine. The chef, as you all know, is the seed that will grow your sourdough starter. We have used organic stone-ground flour and spring water to form the chef," the speaker said as the first rows of ARTOS bakers got up and went up to the front of the room to look at the various specimens.

Heaven pulled another copied page from the bottom of the pile in front of her. This list looked a little more promising: The causes of necrosis, or dead tissue, were varied. Heaven recognized about half of them, reasons like brown recluse spiders, cobras, and rattlesnakes. There were a few surprises such as Tylenol and sea anemone and several words Heaven wasn't familiar with. The Tylenol surprised her the most. Could the general have overdosed on over-the-counter pain relievers until his tongue turned black and gone off the grain elevator like a stock trader during the depression?

"One of the hardest things about the use of sourdough is maintaining the chef so you don't have any days of down time when you have no sourdough. For the home baker this isn't usually crucial but for us, it can mean a loss of revenue. We all know that to maintain your chef you must add more water and flour to the original. But how much flour and how much water? Now is the time for you to get out your calculators and I will show you my simple formula," the speaker said as he flipped on an overhead projector and a screen filled with figures.

Heaven had been circling the words she needed to look up on the necrosis list. The sound of bakers shuffling in their chairs for paper and pencils and calculators brought her back to the task at hand. She crammed her library papers in her bag and brought out the appropriate tools, paper, pencil, and calculator. She really did want to learn to make sourdough, really.

Murray drove down the avenue that led from the area around Kansas State University to the Riley County Hospital, where Diane had told him he would find the county coroners office and the morgue. Diane had turned into a fount of information. She had assured a testy assistant that Murray should be treated with respect. Murray had, in turn, asked Diane to have lunch with him, after his tour of the lab, of course.

Murray had a feeling about the general now, he had a mental picture of the man. From what he had learned, Murray wasn't leaning in the direction of the general committing suicide, that was for sure. The general Diane described was confident, focused, driven. He was a stickler for details, like proper maintenance of equipment. If it turns out that there was a malfunction of the elevator lift, Diane said, it won't be a mechanical problem. No, Diane insisted, it will be a human problem, someone tampering with the lift.

Murray wouldn't go along with Diane on the conspiracy theory yet, but he did know something wasn't right. He decided to try his luck with the coroner.

As Murray circled the hospital he spotted a separate door marked Coroner's Office. Taking bereaved relatives in where living patients were still fighting for life must have seemed too cruel to the city fathers of Manhattan, Kansas. Murray parked as close as he could and headed for that door. It surprised him when the door was unlocked, leading to a neat, tidy waiting room. Maybe no one wants to physically attack the medical examiner around here, Murray thought, remembering a bad case he covered in New York where a medical examiner was mutilated. Murray pushed a buzzer next to a reception window.

Heaven walked toward the front of the production room, heading for Dieter and Pauline. The group had a ten-minute break, then they were going to make sourdough starter with the finished chef, and eight or ten hours after that, they could finally make a loaf of bread.

Heaven slid into a chair beside Dieter. "Now I understand why this conference has to last five days," she said. "It takes that long to get one batch of sourdough bread baked."

Pauline and Dieter smiled the knowing smile of experienced bread bakers. "Time is an ingredient, just like the man says," Pauline said with only a slight air of condescension. "Oh, Heaven," Pauline continued, "look at these photos of yesterday's disaster. One of the pastry chefs took them and has already sold one to the Associated Press."

Heaven looked down at the stack of snapshots. The one on top, the showstopper, was of the general in midair, toppling to his death. "Boy, it takes the nerves of a war correspondent to take photographs at a time like this. It's a good shot though. It should make a front page or two." Heaven pulled the stack of photos over in front of her. "What else have we got here?" she asked idly.

Dieter and Pauline weren't paying attention to Heaven. They were already gabbing, deep into a comparison of wheat and rye sourdough. They had either gotten past the moral dilemma of photographing someone on his way out of this life or they never had those kinds of confusing thoughts in the first place.

Heaven looked at the images of panic after the fall, the grain pouring down on the general, Dieter looking like a superhero digging through the grain to uncover the body, the two assistants who had shoveled the wheat out of the truck, frozen in time in their hazmet suits and their breathing masks. Heaven picked up that shot, looking hard at the two men. In that getup, you couldn't really tell who they were, but Heaven did remember only one of the guys driving the truck away from the elevator before the accident. Maybe the other masked man stayed behind to jimmy the elevator lift.

It was the eyes. The eyes of one of the masked men gave Heaven a vague feeling of remembrance. The eyes looked familiar. Quickly, Heaven glanced at Dieter and Pauline to make sure they weren't watching her. They weren't. Heaven slipped the snapshot into her bag. It wasn't a good composition and it didn't have the victim front and center, so she was willing to chance that the photographer, whoever that was, wouldn't miss one shot from a thirty-six exposure roll. She wanted to look at those eyes once more with a magnifying glass.

Murray, where the hell have you been?" Heaven yelled out the pass-through window where diners' orders would soon be grabbed by frantic waiters. It was only six in the evening but Murray usually showed up between four-thirty and five so he could get the lay of the land, as he put it, before it got busy. Friday night was always busy.

Murray walked into the lion's den—the kitchen—and grabbed a crisp green bean and chomped. "As a matter of fact, my fair leader, I've been in Manhattan, Kansas. I don't know what happened. I think I must have been kidnapped by those aliens you always hear about. I was on my way to 43rd Street and the next thing I know, I'm at the Milling and Grain International Studies Laboratory. Fascinating place. I loved the fat-free donut girls."

Heaven had stopped working after the first sentence. She was jumping up and down in place, looking very excited. Her red hair was glowing and the spikes were bouncing. "Murray, you dog. I got sourdough 101 and you got to go sleuthing. Somehow I think you got the best end of the deal. What did you find out?"

"Well, I thought I might have to come back to Kansas City empty-handed. Oh, I got an impression of him, the general, at the lab. And I had lunch with the receptionist, and she gave me more big-picture stuff. Seems this alliance with BIG BREAD has brought in a boatload of cash for the lab."

Heaven squinted her eyes, as if she could see Manhattan, Kansas, if she squinted. "So, how does that fit in to the, quote, accident, end quote?"

Murray bit into another green bean. "That's just it. The general and BIG BREAD didn't seem to have a beef. They were still on a business partner's honeymoon. This new breakthrough with the perennial wheat could make everyone very rich, at least that's the impression I got from Diane, the receptionist."

"Did they tell you any more about the perennial wheat?"

"Oh, no. The fellow who worked closely with the general and who took me on the five-cent tour was very close-mouthed. I even mentioned that I had heard rumors about this tremendous new strain of wheat and that my editors were very interested in such topics. He said any talk of a new genetic strain was very premature, that much more testing had to be done first."

Heaven smacked her Chinese cleaver down hard on the work table, smashing garlic cloves in the process. "I knew it. I knew the general was just saying that stuff about perennial wheat to get Walter Jinks in an uproar. They probably don't have a . . ."

Murray jumped in. "Oh, I think they are working on it. Diane knew all about it so it couldn't be in the top-secret stage. I think everyone is telling a little of the truth. Yesterday, the general announced something that is still in the experimental stage because he wanted to look good to the star bakers and, yes, to get Walter Jinks where he lives. My tour guide was being cautious and yes, there most likely is more testing to be done before this thing is ready to be planted worldwide. Diane hears the scuttlebutt in the employee lunchroom and sees dollar signs and yes, it will make money for whoever controls it eventually."

"Oh, and I forgot the news we heard at the Board of Trade today. BIG BREAD has applied for a patent for the wheat clone," Heaven said, squinting her eyes again.

"That could be because of what happened yesterday. Even if they weren't ready to patent this, this plant, after the general spilled the beans they were trying to cover their ass."

Heaven looked hopefully at Murray. "And they were so mad at him, and there is so much money at stake, they killed him."

"Nah, that's not how I see it. I think we should check out the arrangement between the International Grain lab and the BIG BREAD guys, but my nose for news doesn't itch. Aren't you going to ask me if I saw the killer elevator?"

"Murray, I know you saw it, by hook or by crook. Which was it? I bet the powers that be kept you away but you snuck around when everyone was at lunch. Did you find anything?"

Murray shook his head. "Wrong on both counts. The powers that be thought I was a reporter for the *New York Times* who had a legit appointment with the general."

Heaven threw a green bean in Murray's direction. "Well, that's the truth now, Mr. Letters from the Interior. Nothing could be more interior than the breadbasket of the country and Manhattan, Kansas, is right in the middle of it. So what if you didn't get the idea to write about this until the general was dead. The lab folks don't need to know that."

"I told them I had to tell the story like it was today, not how it would have been last week. I needed to talk about how the top man died, didn't I? The team leader, who had worked with the general when they were both in the army, took me out back, showed how the gizmo works, wheat goes in below, then up and in the silos. He rode up the very same lift that the boss man rode up, it worked like a charm."

"They could have replaced the broken parts," Heaven shot back. She wasn't ready to give up on the BIG BREAD patent death theory.

"There was still a policeman on duty. There was a police guard all night. The policeman said his boss, the lieutenant, had taken the lift to the top himself, no problems. The guard was staying right there until a team of experts from the elevator company got there to check it out." Murray had a grin on his face that wasn't compatible with the sad subject of their conversation.

Heaven saw the smile. "OK, buddy. If it's not a hitch in the elevator, and it's not the patent-stealing corporate meanies, who is it?"

Murray held up both hands. "Oh, I don't have this thing solved, not by a long shot. After the lab, I went to call on the Riley County coroner. He doesn't have all the tests back, of course. Said he had to send things up here to Kansas City to the regional lab. He could tell me about all the broken bones, that the general had been in good health before his death, that he didn't have a brain tumor or an enlarged heart. But there was one thing very off, and the coroner was very troubled by it."

Heaven came around the table with a menacing look in her eye. The cleaver was still in her hand. "Will you please spit it out. I'm running out of time and patience. By the way, I found out today those are two things you need to be a bread baker."

"Give up on the bread, Heaven, if time and patience are requirements," Murray said with a grin. He realized he better spill the beans. "Okay, okay. The general was tripping on acid."

Silence for a good five seconds. "LSD? *That* acid?" Heaven couldn't believe it but it certainly explained the flying thing. "How can he, the doc, be so sure?"

"One thing led to another, he said. Understand he didn't open up his heart to me. I told him I'd been sent to do a profile on the general and his work and now I had ended up with a mystery. I asked him what he knew and he told me on the condition I wouldn't print the LSD news until he had all the test results in. He said lysergic acid diethylamide was the last thing he had expected to find and he wanted to be sure, get a second opinion. I agreed to not spill the beans until he had corroboration."

Heaven hugged Murray around the neck with the cleaver still in her hand. "This is big, Murray. You have really brought us some big news. Now why was the general tripping? Do you think he was a human guinea pig, doing those experiments like Timothy Leary used to do?"

Murray unwound Heaven from him and slipped the knife out of her hand. It wasn't that he didn't trust her but she did tend to gesture wildly when she got excited. And she was definitely excited. "Maybe, babe. But you remember—thank God it never happened to me—but remember that people used to dose other people with LSD, people who didn't know they'd been dosed. Maybe the ol' general was slipped the stuff. We don't know how he got it, just that he got it." Murray couldn't help grinning that grin again. "But, I will say this, I almost grabbed that coroner and danced around the room with him, I was so excited. I know this is at least part of the reason the general thought he could walk on air."

"That explains the look on his face that I couldn't explain. He wasn't scared a bit. He really thought he could walk on air." Heaven looked at her watch and then the rest of the kitchen staff. They had fallen strangely silent for so early in the shift. They usually didn't shut up until they felt the strain of being slammed, which usually occurred about eight in the evening. Then she realized the conversation between her and Murray was juicy enough to shut up this gabby crew. "It may not be the answer to everything, like how could anyone but the general time his dose so he would be out of his mind at just the right time, when he was fifty-feet high on the silo. And that seems to eliminate our chief suspect, Walter Jinks."

Murray looked puzzled. "From what you've said about Walter, he was around for the LSD days. Why would this eliminate him?"

"I know, Murray, anything is possible, BUT . . . Walter and the general didn't have their falling out until minutes before the accident. The LSD had to have been in his system for a couple of hours, if my memory serves me right. Murray, did the coroner say anything about necrosis?"

Murray was heading for the door to the dining room. He stopped and turned back toward Heaven, wagging his finger at her. "What made you ask that? You knew, you little devil!"

"I only knew that I saw the tip of the victim's tongue and it was black. I didn't know it was necrosis, or what it was. I just got a little research material today. Of course, if I'd known you were going off to investigate I might have mentioned it, you little devil yourself. Come on, what did the doc say about necrosis?"

"Well, he didn't tell me about the tongue, thank you very much. He just said there was some dead tissue, necrosis, on the extremities. Were the general's fingers black too?"

"I didn't look at his fingers, Murray. I didn't even want to see his tongue, for God's sake, it just happened. Do you think the two things have anything to do with each other?"

Murray shrugged. "The LSD and the black extremities, you mean? Don't know, babe. This'll send us back to the library, that's for sure. But right now, we've got people to feed, money to make. I thought you were going to some wing-ding with the bread gang tonight."

"I'm going, I'm going, but not for an hour or so. Tonight is the usual barbecue extravaganza that every visiting chef wants when they're in Kansas City. The whole world has heard about Kansas City barbecue. They're tasting at four restaurants and I'm catching up with them at the third. I asked Pauline to call me when they were headed to R.G.'s."

"R.G.'s is your favorite. I love his beans. Take care and call me later so I can tell you what a great job everyone did," Murray said as he left the kitchen.

It was almost two hours later when Pauline called, sounding like she had already downed a few beers along with the brisket and ribs. They were on their way to R.G.'s and was Heaven still going to meet them? Yes, Heaven said. She would check the front and be right along. She gave her final instructions to the kitchen staff and hit the doors to the dining room.

Bobby Short was singing Cole Porter on the sound system, the guests and staff seemed to be strangely in sync with one another, the bar was filling up with the second seating. It was just after eight, early enough that Heaven could see three turns of the tables tonight for the dining room, if the late reservations were good. She ambled over to the front desk, which wasn't a desk at all, but the end of the bar closest to the door. It was here that Murray presided, reservation book and menus ready.

"Tonight looks promising, Murray. Everything okay? What's the last turn like?"

Murray studied the reservation book with one eye and the room with the other eye. Even though Murray wasn't a true restaurant professional, the fact that he could judge the dining room so well was what made him great at his job. It was a gift that no amount of training could teach. How does a person know when the couple in the corner needs their check, when the birthday party in the center of the room needs their birthday cake brought out at just the right time? How does someone sense when the couple at the bar is getting tired of waiting for a table and needs a free drink to stay put? Murray had the gift. Heaven was afraid that soon Murray would be too busy with his writing to work at the cafe, but until then, she rested easier when Murray was at the door.

"We have eighty reservations after nine. That's almost a full turn so the joint's jumping tonight. We may be able to pay for those new microphones Chris and Joe want."

Just then Chris Snyder ran up to Heaven. "I know you're trying to leave but please come over to that deuce. They had their first date here last year, and he just gave her an engagement ring, tonight, at that table. They seem to think you're responsible."

Heaven groaned. "And they'll think that when its time for the divorce and property division, too. I hate it when we bring couples together. It's so dangerous. But we need to treat them with something. Have they had champagne?"

"Two bottles of Veuve Clicquot," Chris said.

"Well, they don't need any more booze then. How about a dessert pu-pu platter? I'll tell the kitchen to fix up an assortment."

"That sounds good because they're almost done with their entrees. But I really need you to go by the table," Chris said firmly. He knew his tip would increase if he could get Heaven to bless the new couple.

Bless them she did, and then even remembered to order their free desserts on the way out the back door.

Heaven walked toward her van in the darkness, her head full of thoughts, everything from the sanctity of marriage to LSD to sourdough chefs and the sourdough bakers as well. All of a sudden, a loud noise on the other side of her van made her jump. A huge possum trundled in front of the garbage dumpster, hissing in her direction. It had evidently knocked over a stack of plastic pails. She clapped her hands and shouted. "You pea brained sloth. Get away. You scared me half to death."

As Heaven got in her van, more sounds erupted from the dark side of her van, this time they were the distinct sounds of a person running away. She didn't see anyone, just heard the steps.

"Oh, my God. What's going on . . ." She knew she should go back in and have someone check out the area behind the dumpster, but lots of people went up and down the alley and Heaven's van had been broken into only once. She didn't want the delay that would definitely occur if she went back in the restaurant and said someone had been out behind the van in the alley. She started the motor instead. She had backed up and pulled out of the alley on to 39th Street before she sensed something was different in her van. For one thing, the seat had been moved. She could barely reach the brake pedal. As she pulled over to the side of the street and adjusted her seat, she realized that someone had been in her car. Not only had her seat been moved but the plastic dairy case that rested between the two front seats was clear in the back of the vehicle.

That dairy case, a crate that was used to deliver gallons of milk or quarts of cream to a restaurant or grocery store, was usually full of mail that Heaven picked up at her post office box, magazines, letters from wineries, an occasional cookbook. Heaven tried to remember sending someone with longer legs from the restaurant on an errand in the van, but she knew good and well she hadn't done that. She turned the ignition off and turned to peer into the back of the van. Somehow she knew the dairy case would have something in it or on it that hadn't been there a few hours before when Heaven had last driven the van.

Sure enough, there was a longish plastic container sitting on top of the crate. Heaven snagged the dairy case with one foot and pulled it toward her.

"Well, I guess we know what the phantom in the alley was doing," Heaven muttered to herself.

What if it was a bomb, or one of those spring devices that sent acid spraying on your face? She knew she should go back in the restaurant with the container, or at least that she shouldn't open it sitting alone in the dark in her car. She knew all that but opened it anyway. Inside was a loaf of BIG BREAD. It had been ripped open down the top with a serrated bread knife, which had been left sticking out of the bread, jagged pieces of plastic wrapping caught on the blade. The BIG BREAD logo and the polka dots that bordered the package were pulled apart violently. There was a blotch of red on the bread that looked like blood. It gave Heaven a chill but she didn't for a minute think it was blood. She had seen this food-as-blood trick before. Carefully she dabbed the red stuff on her little finger and carefully licked it off. It was raspberry preserves. Heaven stared at this bizarre centerpiece for a moment before seeing a piece of paper stuck on the knife deep in the gummy heart of the loaf of bread. She started to pull out the knife, and even as she did it she heard her friend, Detective Bonnie Weber, screaming "fingerprints, you idiot," in her mind. Heaven pulled the edge of her jacket sleeve down on her palm and grabbed the knife with the protected hand, laying it carefully on the floor.

This time, curiosity won out over good police procedure and Heaven snatched the scrap of paper free. It had two words written in pencil in boxy letters, STOP THEM. Heaven assumed the them was BIG BREAD, the makers of the bread the note had been stuck to. But maybe it had a broader application, to the ARTOS group, who after all, also made bread. Maybe the culprit couldn't stand the idea of spending five bucks for a loaf of bread he was just going to push a knife in, so he got a cheap loaf for the prank.

Whichever group the warning was for, why was it left in Heaven's van?

Scones

2 cups flour
3 T. sugar
1 T. baking powder
½ tsp. kosher salt
8 T. cold butter
3 eggs
3 T. heavy cream
Zest of 1 orange
¾ cup currants

Mix all the dry ingredients. Blend in cold butter in table-spoon size pats until the mixture is pea-sized crumbs. Mix and stir together eggs and cream and zest. Add wet ingredients to dry until the dough comes together. Add the currants. The dough will be wet. Knead lightly on a floured surface. Roll out to 1-inch thick. Cut dough with round pastry cutter or into triangles. Freeze cut dough for 15 minutes or overnight. Brush the tops with a beaten egg to which a tablespoon of cream has been added. Bake at 350 degrees, 15–25 minutes, until golden brown.

Nine

At R.G.'s, aromatic meat smells and smoky air hung heavy in the room, mixing with rhythm and blues from the juke-box. Tonight the room was raucous and crowded, packed as it was with bread bakers and the usual locals. Although R.G.'s wasn't known nationally like Arthur Bryant's and Gate's and KC Masterpiece, it was one of those hidden gems that locals like to keep to themselves. When the host committee for the ARTOS conference started planning this night of barbecue, Heaven had been tempted to keep quiet about R.G.'s. But this conference wasn't a bunch of doctors or funeral directors. These were food professionals. They needed to taste the best, and in Heaven's opinion that was R.G.'s.

Heaven was glad to get to a room full of people after the creepy discovery in her car. As the warmth and the music and the laughter washed over her, she suddenly realized that one of these ARTOS folks could be responsible for her little surprise. But which of these out-of-town bakers could have slipped away to wander around town, find her restaurant, identify her car and leave the bread, then slip back to join the group? Either they all did it as a group project, bus driver please wait a minute, or someone closer to home was responsible, someone who already knew where Cafe Heaven was.

"Heaven, over here!" It was Pauline, with the ever-present Dieter at her side. Heaven gave out a few hugs as she made her way to the table. She plopped down and went right to work on temporarily getting rid of Dieter.

"Oh, boy, am I glad to be here. How were the other two places? Wait, before we do another thing, Dieter, my darling, would you get me something to drink? I don't like beer so I guess orange or strawberry soda is the next best thing in a barbecue joint," Heaven batted her eyes a couple of times just to make sure Dieter understood she expected him to play the gentleman.

"Nonsense, you will drink beer, not some sweet soda pop," Dieter said with a huff. "They have many choices. I'll get you something European." With that, the handsome baker headed toward the bar.

"If R.G.'s has European beer I'll eat my hat," Heaven cracked. "So, Pauline, what's going on with you and your sidekick Tonto?"

Pauline pulled on the bangs of her dark Dutch-boy cut hair and grinned. "First of all, I'll have you know that R.G.'s has Heineken. And the situation with Dieter is very strange. Not that I mind being accompanied around by a handsome and famous German baker. I've met everyone who is anyone, and they're nice to me because Dieter likes me. I even got a job offer from Amy, you know, Amy's Bread in New York."

"Where is she? I'll tear her hair out for messin' with my

Pauline," Heaven said. "Unless you have been harboring a secret desire to move to New York?"

Pauline shook her head. "No, but it made me feel good to be asked. But here's the weird thing about Dieter. Even though he hangs with me all the time he hasn't really flirted or come on to me at all."

"Well, there's always the possibility he's happily married," Heaven said without much enthusiasm.

"Oh, come on boss, he's halfway around the world. Most happily married guys think there's a three-mile limit on their marriage license. Do you think he's gay?"

Heaven eyed the back of Dieter's head at the bar. "Maybe he needs to stay close to you for some other reason, like that he's a spy, and he's using you as a decoy."

Pauline eyed her boss suspiciously. "Are you OK?"

"I know, I know, its my overactive imagination again. Why do I always have to look for some ulterior motives? He could be all of the above, a married gay man who's a spy, but he still chose the best woman to hang with at this conference." Heaven gave Pauline a big hug. She didn't want Dieter's not hitting on her to make Pauline feel less than desirable. Heaven knew from experience that if there's a way a man's problem can be your fault, most women will find the way. She also needed to warn Pauline.

"Honey, I'm going to talk fast before Dieter gets back. Someone put a loaf of BIG BREAD in my car with a knife stuck in it and a note with a warning on it. I want you to be very cautious of everyone. Did Dieter or anyone else show up late for the first barbecue stop? Did anyone ask you where the cafe was? I know we're having a party there on Sunday, so I guess that question could be normal curiosity, but . . ."

Pauline, if she hadn't exactly sobered up, was listening intently to Heaven. "We did have a conversation with that BIG BREAD guy, Dieter and I and a couple of other people," she said. "At Gate's. Dieter was asking Patrick Sullivan all about Cafe Heaven, and he said nice things. I think they talked about where it was located but I don't remember anyone disappearing. Heaven, gosh, now that I think of it I don't remember seeing either of them at the first stop, at Bryant's. I wondered where Dieter was. I didn't really miss Patrick, but I don't remember seeing him."

Heaven looked around the room. She spotted Patrick Sullivan at a nearby table and got up. "I'll be back," she mumbled to Pauline.

Heaven put on her best smile as she sat down beside Patrick. "Well, Mr. Sullivan, how are you weathering this particular storm?"

Patrick Sullivan pushed his glasses up on his nose. "I may jump soon. The shark-infested water has never looked better. I have made progress, however. In the beginning, no one would speak to me. Now I can't get them to stop asking me questions, like how can I live with myself, what do we mean by applying for a patent for a grain, what do we have in mind for taking over the bread market in Mexico from BIMBO. That last question came from a woman bread baker from Spago in Mexico City."

"Patrick, Patrick, Patrick. It's hard being the front man for the evil empire. At least you aren't sitting off in the corner by yourself. By the way, I'm looking forward to the tour of your facility tomorrow. You must admit, the two days this crowd has been in our little town have been action-packed. Surely the demise of the general must have taken the heat off you. By the way, I haven't been able to be at all the meetings today. What's the scuttlebutt?"

He shook his head. "I'm not exactly confidante to the bread stars. But I guess you could say yesterday gave them something else to think about for a while, what with Walter Jinks and the general and the incident, as I like to call it now. So far they have behaved more like paparazzi than artisan bakers. They all hit the one-hour photo place and immediately developed their gruesome snapshots of the poor general hitting the dirt."

Heaven had completely forgotten about the photo she had pinched at the sourdough lecture. She must remember to look at it with her photo eyeglass as soon as she got home. "So, you find their behavior distasteful, they find yours reprehensible. Its a small world, isn't it? Listen Patrick, we may have a problem."

"Now what's happened?"

"I just got a loaf of bread, your bread, stabbed with a big knife, smeared with raspberry preserves to look like blood, and with a note that said STOP THEM. I think they meant your company."

Patrick Sullivan buried his face in his hands. "First of all, it's not my company. I'm a chef who loved baking bread just like everyone here. I worked for a hotel, loved cooking. One day I wrote a nasty letter to BIG BREAD, about how they owed the little children something better than these loaves full of air and chemicals that they pretend is bread. They called me up and said why didn't I come to work for them and do something about it. That was seven years ago."

"And have you made a difference?"

"What do you think?"

"I haven't seen any healthier, more nutritious loaves with the BIG BREAD label. But you are in research and development, so maybe those are a year or two away from the supermarkets, eh? I'm willing to give you the benefit of the doubt for a while. Now onto another question—the silly still life in my van. Did Dieter ask you about the location of my restaurant?"

Patrick shook his head. "Nah, nothing that particular, just what was the food like, the regular stuff. We talked about the party at your place Sunday night, about how we're looking forward to it, that is, if any of us are still on our feet by then."

"Don't jinx it, babe." Heaven got up and patted Patrick's arm as she walked away.

Heaven looked around for Dieter, but didn't spot him, so she went to the bar herself and got a Diet Coke. For the next thirty minutes she schmoozed the crowd. Everyone was in high spirits and the state of shock of twenty-four hours ago had disappeared. It was easy to dissociate from the gruesome scene they had witnessed. After all, it wasn't as if anyone in ARTOS was responsible, and the possibility that it was an accident made it easy to file away in the back of the brain somewhere. Heaven had trouble getting anyone to speculate about the general's death. Beer and barbecue were preferable to reality. As the crowd got up to go to their final stop of the night, Heaven joined Pauline again.

"Where's Dieter?"

Pauline looked around the room. "I don't know. He brought this beer back for you but I was talking to someone and I haven't seen him since. Heaven, are you going to Blues and Cues with us? I hear they have a great blues/gospel singer tonight."

Heaven shook her head. "No, I think I'll go home early for a change. And you, young lady, don't forget that you have to go in at the crack of dawn and get the bread going before we go to the hotel for Dieter's speech. Don't stay out too late."

Pauline rolled her eyes. "It's only ten-thirty. I can catch a set of music and still be home by midnight. Why don't you come along, H.? You're usually the last one to quit."

Dieter walked in the front door of R.G.'s and looked surprised to see the two women standing there.

"Where have you been?" Heaven asked.

"It's hot and smoky in here. I don't smoke anymore so the smoke bothers me. I just had to get some air, that's all." Dieter looked at his watch. "I want to go to the blues place but I can't stay long. I have to go over my notes for tomorrow. I'll go on the bus, then take a cab to the hotel. Come with us, Heaven."

Heaven looked around at the happy crowd and remembered that she hadn't asked a key question. "I want to go home and see my daughter. She'll be leaving soon to go back to England, to college."

Dieter looked interested. "Ah, yes. Your daughter has a famous father, I hear."

"Dennis still does make the cover of *Rolling Stone* once in a while. By the way, speaking of famous, I guess we lost our famous grain guy. I haven't seen Walter Jinks today, have you?"

Dieter and Pauline both shook their heads. "I hope poor Mister Jinks didn't get arrested," Pauline said. "I know he didn't mean stopping the general like that, or at least, well, I don't think he meant it like that. Well, you know what I mean."

They all started walking toward the door. "I know what you mean, Pauline. I'm rooting for Walter to save the world myself. What about Ernest Powell? Did he show today?"

Dieter knew the answer to that one. "He told me yester-day he had a field to plow, and he would come up to the city, as he so quaintly put it, for the weekend. Said he would say his piece after I was done on Saturday at lunch."

As the bakers headed for the buses, Heaven hugged Pauline and winked at Dieter over Pauline's shoulder. "Dieter and Ernest. What a program to look forward to. Bye, you two. Be good," she said as she headed for the van.

Even though she had disturbed the still life and note in her car, she hadn't thrown it in the trash when she got to R.G.'s. It had seemed like the kind of thing that would attract attention if anyone saw her walking to the Dumpster with it, so she had just left it in the van, to show to Murray or Hank before she threw it away. It wasn't threatening personally, but it was disturbing.

When she got in the van, she did so cautiously. The dairy case was nowhere to be seen, and Heaven assumed it had slid to the back of the van when she parked. But soon a movement from the back made her realize that wasn't what had happened. As her eyes adjusted to the dark, she stood up and walked to the back of the vehicle to see what had tipped over. Another quick movement made her freeze in place, then stumble and fall onto the passenger seat before just barely grabbing the edge of the armrest to balance herself. Her first scream was already in the air.

The last reluctant bakers getting on the buses paused and looked around, trying to figure out where the screams were coming from. From the second row of bus seats, Pauline recognized Heaven's voice and jumped off, pulling Dieter behind her. The bus driver and several others followed her charge across the parking lot. When they got to the van, Heaven was sitting on the pavement waving her hands. "Get them out, get them out, get them out," she screeched. The doors of the van were closed. Pauline headed toward the driver's door.

"In the back. Get them away," Heaven whimpered, losing her momentum as more people arrived. She buried her head in her hands. Pauline ran to the side door and jerked it open. Heaven wanted to tell her to let someone else do it but she couldn't make the words come fast enough. She closed her eyes tight and waited to hear the scream. Right on cue, Pauline screamed and ran around to Heaven, burying her head on Heaven's shoulder. The rest of the rescuers were momentarily silenced by the scene.

Someone had added to the bread tableau in the back of the car. A pile of wheat had been tossed on top of the case and the open loaf of bread. And two live rats were having a feast, chowing down on the grain and the bread. Perched on top of the pile, one of the rodents had raspberry jam smeared bloodlike in the darkness on his face. When the side door opened, the rats had tried to retreat to the farthest corner of the van. But their legs were unsteady and they couldn't scamper down the sides of the plastic dairy case. Instead, they wobbled and collapsed on top of the pile of grain.

The bus driver had run into the restaurant and come out with a broom. He snagged the case and pulled it out of the van, toppling everything onto the parking lot pavement. A new low-fat cookbook, several manila envelopes, and the electric bill for the restaurant, all spilled out along with the bread, the wheat, and the rats. Heaven couldn't help herself. She got up and moved to the other side of the van, where the debris from the crate landed. The rats convulsed several times and then lay still, apparently dead.

Peanut Butter Shortbread

1 ½ cups unbleached all-purpose flour
½ cup firmly packed brown sugar
½ cup white sugar
½ cup cornstarch
½ tsp. salt
2 sticks (16 T.) cold unsalted butter, cut in cubes or slices
½ cup smooth peanut butter
1 tsp. vanilla

Mix dry ingredients by hand or in a food processor. Add butter, peanut butter, and vanilla until the dough comes to-gether. It will be crumbly. Pat dough into a lightly buttered 13 × 9-inch pan. Bake for 35 minutes at 325 degrees. Keeps up to 2 weeks in an airtight container.

Ten

Iris and Heaven sat on the bed together. The television was on but they weren't really watching it. They had a legal pad and a newspaper and a reference book spread out in front of them along with a tray of snacks. They had been looking up relevant information on how much BIG BREAD's stock was selling for and on patent law.

"Honey, these cookies are delicious," Heaven said. "Peanut butter shortbread is Kansas City and London all mixed up together. Did you make this up?"

Iris grinned, proud to have praise for her baking from her Mom. "Yes I did. You know how much I loved peanut butter cookies when I was little. I just mixed their shortbread with my peanut butter. The tea bags love them, even if they are nontraditional. I made a batch of these today at the restaurant. They were going to serve them with the sorbet and ice cream assortment tonight."

"Do you call the English 'tea bags' in front of your father? I bet he has a fit," Heaven chuckled.

"Oh, Mom, it's an old rock 'n' roll term. As you very well

know. Dad's been hearing tea bag his whole life. Besides, I really have to push Dad to get him mad, push him farther than calling him a tea bag, that's for sure."

"I know, honey. You can do no wrong as far as your father goes. And as far as I go, of course."

"Don't lie, Mom. I know you've got my number. And I've got yours. I could just kick your butt for driving home by yourself after that horrible rat thing happened. Why didn't you call? I could have come after you."

"And I would have come with her," Hank said as he came up the stairs into the bedroom. He pulled off a pair of work gloves and stripped off his shirt. His hair wasn't in the ponytail he wore to the hospital, but was flowing free, black and shining. "The car is cleaned up, inside at least. I left your mail down on the table. Some of it is kind of sticky, I guess from the jam. It will dry off. Now I'm going to jump in the shower."

Heaven got out of bed and gave Hank a kiss, not mushy because her daughter was watching, but at least on the lips. "No one else in the world would have put on their grubby clothes and gone to the garage in the middle of the night and got out the vacuum to clean rat shit and wheat from their girlfriend's car."

Hank put his hand in Heaven's hair and gave her spikes a tug. "You had a terrible scare. I know how you hate rodents, even a little mouse. I'm so sorry. You have had some bad times in that car, H. Maybe its time to get a new one," he said and then went into the bathroom.

"What's he talking about, Mom? What else has happened in that van?"

"Oh, someone shot out the passenger window with a gun. No big deal."

"I suppose you were in the car at the time? Did this happen during that barbeque contest murder?"

"Iris, let's not rehash something that happened ages ago. I'm here aren't I, so it couldn't be too bad," Heaven said, eager to get off that subject. "And we have to figure out what's going on right here, right now. This bread conference isn't over until Monday. Lot's more could go wrong. Now, why do we think they put that stuff in my van? Why not in Patrick Sullivan's car or in one of the tour buses? And I can't forget Dieter coming in from outside right before I found the rats. I'm pretty sure he had a guilty look on his face."

Iris leaned back and ate a corn chip. "Well, one reason could be that your car was more convenient. Maybe the buses weren't at the hotel, or the culprit couldn't recognize Patrick Sullivan's car in BIG BREAD's parking lot. The other reason could be that it was meant to scare you off. A few people know you've been involved in some crime solving. And Murray went out to Manhattan today. Maybe someone thought you sent him. As for Dieter, he's only been in this country a couple of days. Where would he get two rats, Mom, and the poison to kill them with?"

"Details, details. I'm not going to rule Dieter out yet. As for me, I haven't done anything that would single me out, not yet, not this time. I behaved myself when we were in Kansas, didn't I?"

"Like a Sunday school teacher."

"I didn't stick my nose in the police business or lecture all the bakers about how the general had a black tongue and was tripping on LSD."

Iris sat up straight. "MOM. What are you talking about? LSD? Oh, my God."

"I'll tell you everything, but first let Hank get out of the shower. I want him to hear this, too. Let's have a bottle of champagne. After all, you'll be leaving soon. We won't have many more midnight sessions like this."

"Stop it, Mom. Don't get mushy on me. We have a lifetime of midnight sessions ahead of us. But it sounds like a great reason for a bottle of . . ."

"Veuve Clicquot, of course," Heaven said as she bounded down the stairs.

As Heaven unwrapped her legs from around Hank's, she felt a glass at the bottom of the bed. "Boy, it's a good thing we use restaurant grade champagne flutes at this house. There seems to be a glass in here with us."

Hank picked up the glass between his toes, grabbed it with the hand that wasn't around Heaven's breast, and put it on the table beside the bed. He pulled Heaven over on top of him and kissed her. "I thought you and Iris were going to laugh yourselves sick. When you started telling stories about when she was in third grade, it was very touching."

"Then Iris went to bed and we turned everything upside down. Most of the pillows seem to be down where the champagne glass was, and the quilt is on the floor. I hope we didn't make too much noise," Heaven said as she kissed Hank's neck.

"You had Yo Yo Ma playing the cello, and Iris had Bob Dylan's son singing on your respective sound systems. I don't think we were louder than that. Heaven, you know what's coming next, don't you?" Hank said softly as he gathered their bed clothes back to the correct positions.

Heaven was already drifting off but she smiled and put her hand out to Hank. "Say it."

"Heaven, please be careful."

"I will if you'll just look at that list of reasons for necrosis before you leave in the morning. The ones with highlighter are the ones I don't know the definition of. You'll probably know them by heart." Heaven rolled over on her side, cuddling up next to Hank.

"Heaven, if anything were to happen to you, I don't know what I'd do," Hank said sternly. It fell on deaf ears. Heaven was asleep.

The next morning, Heaven walked into Sal's barber shop and went straight to the coffee. It was almost nine in the morning and she had been at the restaurant since seven, getting paperwork done before the crews came in. Sal was always busy on Saturday morning, and this was no exception. Most of the 'Naugahyde' and chrome chairs lining the walls were full. Heaven realized she should watch what she said. After all, one of these straight guys could be a BIG BREAD executive.

"What's up, H. I haven't seen you for days," Sal growled.

"I know. This bread conference is very time-consuming. Plus there've been a few complications."

Sal nodded at Heaven in the mirror. "Yeah, I got that from Murray. Just because you can't be bothered to keep a friend up to date, that doesn't mean Murray hasn't." Sal brandished his scissors with extra flair as he trimmed the sideburns of an Elvis look-alike. Not that the guy was an Elvis impersonator, but he still wore the hair style and clothes style of Elvis in his bloated years.

Heaven took the reprimand in stride, knowing she deserved it. "So we were out in Kansas and these two scientists got into it about how to feed the world's population, and one told the other he had to be stopped, and then about thirty minutes later, one of them falls off a grain elevator and dies."

Sal nodded again. "And Murray finds out the dead man was high as a kite on LDC."

"LSD," Heaven corrected. She paused and looked around the room for reaction. After the mention of LSD, everyone had either buried their nose in a magazine or was staring in rapt attention at Sal and Heaven. There was no middle ground. "So a local bread manufacturer is involved in this, and they've applied for a patent. Iris and I looked it up last night and it said Congress can grant exclusive rights to scientists for their discoveries for limited times, which is seventeen years and that doesn't sound so limited to me, of course compared to the history of time I guess it is, limited I mean."

Sal brushed off the Elvis look-alike's neck and took off his cloth wrap. As he always did between customers, he took a quick sweep at the floor around the chair with a broom and long-handled dustpan while Elvis fished for his eight bucks. Sal's was the cheapest haircut in town.

"You're not making sense, H. A patent for what? Some new bread machine?"

Heaven got up and poured more coffee. "Sorry, I'm not telling the story very well. A wheat clone. They're patenting a wheat clone."

Sal looked up with disgust. "Heaven, you must have got some of that LSD. You can't patent food for God's sake. You just said it gives the patent holder exclusive rights. So no one but BIG BREAD could make bread, for God's sake? Don't try that one on me."

"I never said BIG BREAD, Sal. Did I say BIG BREAD, everybody?" Heaven asked the room. Everyone became very interested in the month-old magazines. One young guy in a denim workshirt mumbled no and leered at Heaven. She turned back to Sal.

"Well, the rest of the world couldn't use this particular wheat clone, only the, uh, bread company that will remain nameless could do that. And this wheat clone might turn out to be very valuable. So they would definitely have an unfair advantage over the rest of the world. Maybe. Its complicated. Sal, do you know any patent attorneys?"

Sal had his next customer ready to go, a neighborhood gentleman in his seventies. He walked up to Sal's every Saturday for a trim, which he usually didn't need. It was his exercise, he said. Sal also knew it was his way of getting the neighborhood news. He was sure getting his eight bucks worth today. "What makes a patent attorney?" Sal asked from the back of the chair.

"You have to be a lawyer with a degree in engineering or physical science as well."

Sal shook his head. "Doesn't sound familiar but some lawyers usually come in on Saturdays, I'll check it out."

Heaven got up and reluctantly put her coffee cup in the extra sink and rinsed it out. "I just touched the surface of the subject of patents last night and I have to go to this damn lunch at eleven. Before that I have to spend the rest of the morning in the kitchen, so I can't even go to the library. I have a feeling this is important so if you find out anything, let Murray know. He'll be in around four."

Sal grabbed his first cigar of the day and stuck it, unlit in his mouth. "What's the damn world coming to if you can patent something like wheat? That can't be right, H."

"Sal, you and I both know that big companies don't spend millions of dollars on research to make a product better if they can't earn their money back, even if the product is food. So don't be surprised that you can patent something you shouldn't be able to patent."

Sal reluctantly agreed. "Okay, I get the drift. I'll ask around."

Heaven went back to her side of 39th Street. She felt better. When Sal said he'd ask around, he always got results.

Dieter Bishop couldn't get out of the shower. He knew if he did, he would die. The hot water had been gone for a while now. Dieter was shivering with the icy cold water that was cascading off his face, his back. The monster that was waiting for him outside the shower doors knew he was freezing, that he had to be downstairs in an hour, that he had to give a speech. It knew everything.

Dieter had a brilliant idea. He would bargain with the monster. "Yoo-hoo," Dieter called, as he slid the shower door open a crack and peeked his head out "I'm coming out now. If you just let me go make my speech, I'll do everything you want. Please, everything you want."

There was a roar that made Dieter put his hands up over his ears. Then the bathroom was empty.

Dieter made a stumbling beeline for the bedroom. He was blue from the cold, his body shaking. He fumbled through his suitcase until he found what he was looking for. He removed the syringe and filled it quickly.

Heaven walked into the meeting room at the Ritz-Carlton hotel. The ARTOS bakers had the morning off. Most of them had gone shopping on the fancy Country Club Plaza, right across from the hotel. Heaven and Pauline had been working their butts off so they could have time off for this lunch and for the tour of BIG BREAD that was coming up in the afternoon. They had gone together to the hotel and Heaven let Pauline out at the door and then parked the van. Once inside the conference room she spotted Pauline talking to Dieter and Nancy Silverton from La Brea Bakery in Los Angeles. When the two celeb bakers both moved toward the speaker's table, Pauline found Heaven. They started cruising for a good seat.

"Dieter says hi and so does Nancy. She couldn't believe we drove the rat van here today," Pauline said as they sat at a table near the front of the room.

"Gosh, I'm sorry. The Rolls is in the garage," Heaven replied with a sniff. "Speaking of the rat van, thanks for your help last night. Making me slam that shot of tequila was brilliant. At least I stopped whimpering. I was a mess. I hate rats. I hate mice. I'm deathly afraid of them. Remember last winter when we had mice in the basement of the restaurant?"

"I remember, all right," Pauline said. "We had enough pest exterminators around to delouse all of 39th Street. It was overkill. But what was all that about last night? Why would someone put rats in your van?"

"If they knew me at all, to scare me, I guess."

"Even if you weren't rodent phobic, what was the point? There was a loaf of BIG BREAD, a big old bread knife, fake blood preserves, poisoned rats, and a note that said, what was it?" Pauline was finally getting into the Cafe Heaven investigator mode.

"STOP THEM. That's what the note said."

"And did that mean stop them, the bread company or stop them, the ARTOS bakers, or stop them, the Cafe Heaven crew?"

"Exactly," Heaven said with a smile. "Now you understand why Murray and Chris and Joe and everybody always ask more questions than we give answers when we get on these cases. The note was attached to a BIG BREAD loaf, Pauline. Let's take it at face value and assume that's who has to be stopped, in the opinion of the jolly prankster."

"Then I would say that Walter Jinks is the prime suspect. If BB, that's what I'll say from now on so no one will know who we're talking about, if BB paid for research for the general, and the general beat Walter at his own game, then Walter is the prime suspect." Pauline smiled her superior bread-baker smile.

Heaven smiled her "oh brother" smile back. "The obvious is sometimes the best, eh Pauline? But calling BIG BREAD BB, I think, is a little too obvious. On, the other hand, you are certainly correct about Walter being the obvious choice. That's three things obvious in one fell swoop. Something's wrong."

Pauline frowned. "But Walter wasn't at the ARTOS meetings yesterday."

"It isn't very far from GRIP to Kansas City. Just because he didn't come to the meetings doesn't mean he wasn't in Kansas City. Now hush for a minute and let's try to enjoy lunch."

"Okay, but there he is now, and Ernest too," Pauline said, pleased to get the last word for a change.

Sure enough, Walter Jinks was walking in the door, deep in discussion with Ernest Powell. Why, Heaven wondered, were they always talking to each other when they were on opposite sides of the wheat question? Was it just because they were both from Kansas, both farmers? Another thing to worry about.

The meeting was called to order and lunch was served. The Ritz went a little overboard with the bread theme, but everything tasted good. First there was an onion soup served in a scooped out French roll. Then, panzanella, Italian bread salad of chopped tomatoes, onions, bread, lots of basil, and garlic. The Ritz put a grilled chicken breast on the top of the panzanella to make it an entree salad. Heaven liked her version better. She added olives and chopped cucumbers, walnuts, and sometimes roasted red peppers and white beans, but never chicken breasts, which Heaven thought the most overused item in American restaurants. Dessert was bread pudding, of course.

After lunch it was time for Dieter's treatise on rye. Heaven had watched him push his food around on his plate, not eating. It was cute that he was nervous. The hotshot American bakers could be daunting. As far as she was concerned, he could say anything and she would believe it, she knew so little about rye. Heaven was restless. She was missing vital information, and it wasn't about Dieter's favorite grain.

"My family has been making rye bread for 800 years. For 400 years we have baked professionally in the same bakery I now work in every day," Dieter explained. "Of course we have made quite a few improvements over the years, but the grain, the water, the yeast, they have remained constants. We have had the same coal-burning oven for 200 years. This is a great joy and a great responsibility. I feel my grandfather and his father before him looking out for me and also looking to me to carry on the family tradition. No male in our family has ever turned his back on the baking profession."

Heaven tried to pay attention but her mind had a different idea. When was it that things started going wrong, Heaven wondered? The first thing we did with the ARTOS bakers was the tour of GRIP. Walter told everyone what he was working on and implied that the Mennonites had brought disaster with them in the form of 'Red Turkey' wheat, which grew too well, as well as the disaster of annual crops that stripped the topsoil, according to Walter. Then there was the disaster of depending too much on one type of wheat, if we had to depend on wheat.

Dieter forged ahead. "We have already discussed using a chef, or mother, to create sourdough. The same method is used for rye sourdoughs. The initial chef takes four days to create. The sourdough made with the chef takes eight to ten hours to develop. Then you are ready to make rye sourdough. I have a computer handout with the measurements to give you later."

Heaven looked around the room. She barely knew most of these folks. Oh, of course, she had read about many of them, and read their cookbooks, and even eaten at their restaurants and cooked with them. But she didn't know them, really. She could be looking in the wrong direction for a villain. All of these bakers had been at the scene of the general's so-called accident. As far as she knew, none of them had been at her restaurant or in her car. And by the time the rats were added, they all were at the same place again. A hundred and twenty artisan bakers were too many lives, stories, alibis to deal with. Back to Walter.

"Let's take a moment to talk about rye," Dieter was saying with gusto. "For me in my country, rye is more prominent than wheat as a bread ingredient because rye grows in the wet climate that we have. In the north, breads are still made with one hundred percent rye flour. The closer to Italy, the lighter in color the bread, usually with less than fifty percent rye flour. I make most of my rye sourdough breads with a ratio of sixty percent rye and forty percent wheat flour. Why do I use a rye sourdough at all? Why not just straight yeast breads? Because the rye sourdough adds elasticity and firmness that the bread would not have without it. As you all know, rye does not have gluten."

Heaven looked over at Ernest Powell. He was listening intently to Dieter. Heaven still seemed to remember that the Mennonites had been kicked out of Germany before they went to Russia. Didn't some Russian queen—was it Catherine?—get them to settle in some remote part of Russia? Maybe Ernest was so pro-wheat because those awful old Germans were mean to his people. But Ernest hadn't mentioned hating rye, had he? He did seem a little testy about Walter and his native grasses though. Of course Walter had thrown the first punch on that front.

"Now, a word about enzymes. Enzymes develop in living organisms and function to alter them without altering themselves. In our case, enzymes destroy starch and convert it to sugar. Enzymes are heat sensitive and die at 80 degrees centigrade. In rye flour, the enzymes are active longer than in wheat flour. The enzymes need water to work so many of these enzymes collect in the shell of the grain where the moisture is. So what happens? Enzymes 'chop' water and starches into dextrin. Then the enzymes chop dextrin into maltose sugar. One, two, three," Dieter said briskly. "Because rye flour absorbs water at a lower temperature than wheat flour, rye at 50–60 degrees centigrade as opposed to wheat at 70–80 degrees centigrade, we must add some acidity or sourness to inhibit enzyme activity. Thus, another need for sourdough in rye bread."

Heaven was fascinated with all this rye knowledge. She had actually been sucked into listening by the time he got to the enzymes. If she ever learned to make a decent sourdough with wheat flour, which sounded much easier, she'd give rye a try. Could Dieter be behind all this, sent on a mission from God to destroy the wheat juggernaut? Maybe what she mistook before lunch for stage jitters—Dieter not eating or talking constantly—was actually guilt. It seemed totally ridiculous but the more she learned about the bread game, she saw more worldwide implications and more money involved. People have been dosed with LSD for lesser reasons than a share of the world market for rye flour—if the LSD was actually what killed the general, what made him take the leap.

Dieter had really warmed to his subject. A sheen of sweat covered his face. His eyes glistened with zeal. "Let us sum up the advantages of sourdough in rye bread baking. Number 1, it provides leavening that rye does not have by itself. Number 2, it retains moisture in the finished product. Number 3, it provides the acidity that controls enzyme activity, and Number 4, it adds flavor and aroma. But enough of all this dry talk. Eating is believing. I brought some of my beloved chef, or "mother" as I like to call it, with me to America. I have already baked a few loaves to get the lay of the land here, the water, the native yeasts in the air. And Daniel Leader, of Bread Alone Bakery in upstate New York, has agreed to assist me in making bread for our little party tomorrow night at Cafe Heaven. We will make a complete complement of sourdough ryes including dark pumpernickel with raisins, rye with caraway seeds, rye with potato, a 100 percent whole rye, and the bread I won the Coupe du Monde with, Vollkornbrot, a traditional German bread with whole rye berries. Any of you may join us tomorrow at Home and Hearth bakery for this hands-on workshop."

The audience clapped as if they were at a rock concert, and Heaven looked around for Ernest. He was the encore.

Ernest Powell grinned shyly at the crowd. But his voice was anything but shy. It was strong, confident. "I guess you have been wondering why a wheat farmer from Kansas has to get his two cents worth in at this meeting. I want to tell you my story. My whole life, I woke up to the smell of fresh-baked bread. It symbolizes the home and family to me, and something more. It is a gift from God that the first human fermented grain and water, threw it in the fire and realized that grain could be transformed into this miracle that is bread."

Heaven looked around the room at the heads nodding in agreement. So far, so good. The ARTOS bakers obviously agreed with Ernest.

"Now you all know the chemistry better than me. All I know is, if God hadn't wanted us to have bread, we would still be eating parched corn or gruel. God surely was with that first wife who didn't throw away that piece of sour smelling grain paste but instead baked it on a hot rock. From way before the time of Moses, bread has meant nourishment. I guess they found some evidence of bread in Egypt 4,000 years before Christ. Jesus himself said he was the bread of life. Why, I bet you would agree with me that domesticating cereal plants, my life-long profession, brought us civilization. Those old hunters and gatherers didn't wander so far once they planted a little field of corn."

Ernest was sure up on his grain history, Heaven thought. She looked at Pauline. Rapt attention. Maybe he stood a chance of pulling off this bread-machine project without getting laughed at after all.

"It's kind of funny, that for years, folks thought white bread, made with refined flour, was superior. Those European kings and queens felt the kind of rustic breads that you folks work so hard to make were just for the peasants. Now they're just for those that can afford four and five dollars for a loaf of bread. Nowadays the white bread is for the poor folk."

Heaven saw the troops shift uncomfortably in their chairs. Baking artisan bread had an elitist rep, there was no getting around it. The people who bought artisan breads were hip, savvy, with disposable income.

Ernest continued. "Of course, we know poor folk can't afford four-dollar bread, but they could afford twenty-cent bread. Twenty-cent bread that they could bake in their own home. How in the heck could they do that, you say? With your help, that's how.

"Three years ago I realized we weren't baking bread at our house anymore. My wife is a schoolteacher and, just like in every other busy family, home-baked bread had just fallen by the wayside. So I went out and bought one of those bread-maker machines. Now, hear me out. I know that's not your way of doin' things," Ernest said just before the groans began.

Heaven saw a few eyes rolling, but Ernest was so knowledgeable that he didn't lose the crowd entirely. They were still intrigued. Where was this farmer going with this topic?

"I learned to make bread with this gadget, although I can tell you some of the first attempts were kinda pitiful. But you can't hardly mess up too bad, and the next thing I knew, we had home-baked bread every morning, and for supper, too, if we wanted. I started adding different ingredients, herbs, wheat berries, things like that. To make a long story short, I won the national bread machine contest this year," Ernest said with a proud grin.

The ARTOS bakers clapped appreciatively.

"So I've come to you with an idea, I love bread, but I see how the little guy lives. What if we join together, those of us who grow the wheat, and those who make their living turning it into blessed bread. What if we buy bread machines and give them to those families who may never have smelled that wonderful smell of home-baked bread, who now can set the timer and come home to something they can be proud of. Welfare mothers, single parents, children, will be blessed and so will you if you help me start this foundation." Ernest lowered his eyes, ducked his head and blushed. "I reckon I've talked too long. I thank you for listening," he said quickly and then turned around looking for a way to avoid being the center of attention.

Dieter Bishop was the first to stand up and speak. "Although we probably could use a similar program in Germany, I'd like to leave a thousand dollars here in the United States with Ernest to start this project off. And I challenge all the rest of you rich American bakers to meet my pledge."

That did it. The celebrity bakers couldn't let Dieter shame them. One of the clipboard woman stood by Ernest and wrote down the pledges as the crowd streamed by, shaking Ernest's hand. Ernest looked stunned that the ARTOS crowd had been so agreeable. Heaven figured they all saw the great publicity potential of this. It was a brilliant marketing tactic. Take bread machines to the projects. Get your picture in the newspaper and do good at the same time. What could it hurt?

Pauline pulled at Heaven's arm. "Can we help?"

Heaven stood up and thought a minute. "We sure can't give any thousand dollars. But we can give four hundred, which should buy eight or ten bread machines if we get them wholesale. I'm sure one of the small appliance companies will want to get their picture in the paper, too. Pauline, you go up and make our pledge. Find out where to send the check. I'm going to run down Walter Jinks."

Pauline looked at her boss with alarm. "Run down?" she repeated. "Don't worry," Heaven said. "I'm not violent. I just meant find him and talk to him. Now hurry so we can go on to the bread factory. We'll have to make sure little Patrick Sullivan gives Ernest a check too. BIG BREAD can certainly afford it."

As Pauline headed for Ernest, Heaven looked around for Walter. He was visiting with one of the Acme Bread people. As the two men shook hands and the Californian walked away, Heaven put her hand on Walter's shoulder. "How are you?" she asked gently.

Walter still had a twinkle in his eye. "Heaven, it isn't that bad. You sound like I'm a terminal case of some sort."

"My, you have high tolerance, Walter. Let's see, since Thursday, you've gotten in a public fight with another scientist who then died, I suspect you've been questioned by the police, and the bad guys applied for a patent on something that may render your research moot. Sounds grim to me."

Walter's eyes clouded over for a minute, but then he chuckled and looked Heaven straight in the eye. "Heaven, I suspect you have had adversity in your life as well. Don't tell me a little spot of bad luck would stop you?"

Heaven laughed. "Just in the last few years, since I've had the cafe, I've had a guest die of poisoning, I was almost asphyxiated by a barbeque murderer, and I almost froze to death in a hotel freezer in Aspen. I guess I see your point. But doesn't BIG BREAD's perennial wheat thing the general referred to put your research behind the eight ball?"

"If I thought that was the answer, I would have developed my own strain of perennial wheat. Diversity is the key, Heaven. What if some nasty foreign government, let's say one that doesn't depend on bread, one with a rice-based diet, develops a bug that only eats 'Red Turkey' wheat? Then what will we do?"

"That's basically the situation already according to you, isn't it Walter?"

"The difference is that no one would really bother to develop a poison for an annual. Next year, we start all over, they'd have to send the bugs back."

"But if it's a perennial, oh, I get it. It would take longer to replace the wheat. Bread would then be even more expensive than the stuff these celebrity guys bake. So now I have more things to worry about than I did before Thursday," Heaven said. "In the case of the world grain market, a little knowledge leaves you worried sick. What do you think happened to the general, Walter?"

"Well, as I told the Manhattan detective, he was a man who seemed to be on top of the world. He had a great new mentor in BIG BREAD and he was on the trail of a new discovery. He might have gotten a kick out of getting my goat, but I was no threat to him."

Heaven and Walter had been heading toward the lobby of the hotel with the rest of the group. Dieter and Ernest were in deep conversation about their new bread-machine foundation and were accompanied by lots of bread-machine foundation groupies. Ernest seemed to be adjusting to celebrity quite well.

Heaven turned back to Walter. "But the general was a threat to you, wasn't he?"

Walter laughed. "Do you think that I rigged that lift to pitch the general off the top of the silo? I guess that's what the detective thought as well. What would that get me, pray tell? It wouldn't do away with his research and the folks that financed it, now would it? What you don't understand about me, Heaven, is that I'm in for the long haul. I believe in what I do, and I have for more than twenty years. Remember Leonardo da Vinci? He had to beg and scam the Duke of Milan, or whoever was paying that year, for every penny he had. He stole into the morgue at night to draw dead bodies, to learn anatomy. But we revere him now, Heaven. Some things take more time than others."

Heaven gave Walter a hug. "You are philosophical, Walter. I'm going to read your book, soon."

"*A Grain of Wheat?* I'll send you an autographed copy when our lives get back to normal," Walter said as they walked outside the hotel.

Heaven saw Pauline looking around for her and waved. "So, Walter, you think we will get back to normal after ARTOS?" Heaven asked.

"Remember the long run, Heaven," Walter Jinks said with a mysterious smile.

Heaven's Panzanella

1 loaf day-old French or Italian bread, cut into crouton
    dice and toasted
10 Roma tomatoes, split and sliced
2 red onions, split and sliced
1 cup basil leaves, julienned
1 cup Calamata olives, pitted, or some other good olive
1 cup walnuts, toasted
1 cucumber, split, seeded, and then sliced—I usually peel
    about half the skin off in stripes
1 red pepper, quartered and sliced
1 green pepper, quartered and sliced
1 cup good Parmesan cheese, diced or 1 cup crumbled
    Gorgonzola
Options: 1 cup cooked white beans, 1 cup diced
    cappicola spicy ham, 1 cup sliced salami, 1 tuna filet,
    grilled and cubed
4 garlic cloves, minced, or 6–8 roasted garlic cloves, smashed
Red wine vinegar
Extra virgin olive oil
Kosher salt and freshly ground pepper

Combine everything down to the vinegar in a large bowl.
Drizzle with oil and vinegar, season and let rest for an hour.
Add more oil and vinegar as it will be absorbed by the
bread. Adjust seasonings and serve.

Eleven

BIG BREAD, INC., a sprawling fenced in complex of tile and stainless steel in the middle of Kansas City, rarely received guests. Today, however, the red carpet was out, literally. A red runner rolled out the front door into the parking lot where the buses pulled up. Patrick Sullivan was standing at the doorway of the plant, like a host greeting guests at a formal party. When everyone was off the buses and gathered around the front door, Patrick spoke.

"I know this is a visit to enemy territory for most of you. But I want you to know how much I admire what you have done for bread in the United States. You have brought bread to a much higher profile than it had ten years ago. Many more people know about pain levain, sourdough, ciabatta, and foccacia in America than ever have before. I think you will find this tour interesting, even if you don't approve of the final product. Just remember that we, as food professionals, have to feed the world's population of six billion people. This sometimes calls for assembly-line procedures. So, welcome, to our main bread production facility in the Midwest. We also have a sweet snack cake plant in St. Louis but we have introduced production line flexibility into all our plants, so if the demand was there, we could produce snack cakes here in Kansas City and bread in St. Louis. After the tour, we'll have a little wine and cheese here in the front lobby. Come on into BIG BREAD. We run a small crew on Saturday. The office staff and operations crew are minimal and the line only runs one shift today," Patrick explained, pushing his glasses up on his nose. Heaven had to give credit to the guy. He was being much more gracious than she suspected his guests would ever be to him, or his employers would be if they had to face ARTOS bakers like Patrick did.

As the group trooped into the lobby Patrick diverted them quickly down a corridor. Dieter Bishop held up his hand. "Patrick, where's the john?" He still looked excited, like he had while making the rye speech. Heaven thought Dieter had been very generous to share his spotlight with Ernest and the bread-machine idea.

Patrick pointed in the opposite direction. "Down that hall, Dieter. We'll be over there in the building utilities area."

Heaven touched Dieter's hand as he maneuvered through the crowd. "Great speech. Are you all right?" she asked as she noticed the expression on his face.

"Yes, no, I'll be fine, I . . . I just have to get to the bathroom," Dieter said, looking as though he were going to be sick. Heaven watched him practically run down the corridor.

Patrick was a great tour guide. He made utilities systems positively fascinating. "In this vast room, we have two 275-horsepower screw compressors for the air handling system, a steam boiler, and a separately housed ammonia refrigeration system. We have the capacity to handle twice the current demand. All utility lines are labeled and color coded according to their contents, gas, water, electricity. The layout separates the facility into two zones. The central corridor houses offices, training rooms, and maintenance. On one side are the bays containing the production areas, proofing rooms, raw materials, and the ingredient-delivery system. The other side, where we are now, houses the building systems and receiving and distribution. We have two incoming docks and ten outgoing docks," Patrick explained as they strolled over to the dock area. Today being Saturday, there was nothing happening on the receiving side, but the outgoing docks were about half full of bread trucks loading up.

"The air handling system allows us to control ambient conditions throughout the facility. The makeup and packaging areas are air conditioned, while the oven areas are not. Baking is still a hot job in the summer, even at this sophisticated level."

As the troop straggled down the hall to the other side of the building, Heaven looked around. The group was behaving pretty well. Most of them had never worked in bread factories, as opposed to bread bakeries. It was impressive even if you hated the product it produced.

"We have the most sophisticated ingredient delivery system in the world, bar none," Patrick said proudly. "There are three liquid tanks and four dry bulk silos mounted outside the building. Inside we have these six 8,000-pound major ingredient tanks, then twelve 500-pound minor ingredient tanks, as well as these 25 micro-ingredient bins. They are all equipped with pneumatic feeders and are computer-operated. The minor and micro ingredients are fed into the system through two bag dump stations, networked with the main ingredient system to insure delivery to the proper bin. These color screen terminals on the production area floor provide operator access to the ingredient system." Sure enough, operators were tinkering with dials all over the room. Patrick walked over to one of the screens. "These terminals display current system conditions, showing real-time activities by changing the display color of pipelines and fill levels in the bin diagrams." He walked over to a row of the biggest mixers Heaven had ever seen. "Wet and dry ingredients meet here in these 1,300-pound mixers. When fully mixed, the dough is released from the mixer and dumped in a waiting trough. When the trough is full, a hoist engages it, carries it up and dumps it in a large, wide-feed hopper, right here." Patrick patted a cement mixer–sized hopper, and they watched as a worker brought a trough full of dough over with the hoist and dropped it with a loud splat. "The dough moves down by gravity onto a slow moving conveyor belt that forms the bottom of this feed hopper, as you see. The unstressed dough travels through a series of gauge rollers, then into the next room where the first proofing occurs. We'll go in there in a minute, but because of the heat and humidity, I'll describe the next two processes in here. After approximately eighteen minutes in the primary proofing room, the dough goes on a slow-moving belt through a guillotine cutter and comes out in individual pieces. It is then transferred to a quickly moving transfer conveyer that pulls the dough over and then to a transpositor that drops the dough, piece by piece, row by row, into proofer bread pans on trays. The bread travels on a serpentine path through a Belsaw proofer for another eighteen minutes. The system automatically controls the temperature and humidity within the proofer as well as the speed of the chain carrying the proofer trays."

No wonder these bread companies couldn't be bothered with sourdough. I know it takes hours for sourdough to proof, Heaven thought, and this stuff just takes thirty-six minutes total.

"So we'll peek in the primary proofing room and then pick up the line as it goes through the secondary proofer," Patrick said as they started down the hall. When they opened the doors to the initial proofing room, the heated, humid air hit them, yeasty smelling, with alcoholic overtones, like a brewery. Stainless steel bins like mini dumpsters were lined up in two rows down the middle of the room. When the timer went off, the eighteen minutes were up, and the batch of dough was deposited on another conveyor belt by the whole bin tipping over onto the line.

Patrick pointed up at the air. "The reason this room is entirely automated is the obvious heat—plus the problem of 'dough drunks'. When this much dough is fermented, enough ethanol is produced and released to make the air quite alcoholic. If you worked in here very long, you would have a serious dough drunk. The ethanol, of course, is released every time the dough is effectively 'punched down' by it being released from the bin." The bakers all nodded knowingly. Heaven guessed being dough drunk was something most of them had experienced.

A bell went off and a bin on the opposite side of the room started rising in the air. To everyone's surprise and horror, Dieter Bishop was lying face down in the dough. His blonde hair was unmistakable. Dieter's limp arm and hand hung out of the bin full of dough and dangled over the edge of the conveyer belt. Before anyone could figure out what to do, Dieter's body started moving down the line toward the cutter which came down with a sharp whap every time the dough was sliced into individual loaf size pieces.

Heaven was the first to come out of shock. She reached out as the dough and Dieter passed by, grabbed Dieter's hand and yelled, "Help me get him off before he gets to the guillotine." Patrick had just talked about dough drunks, and she hoped Dieter had just passed out. But if he turned up in the second proofing room in two pieces, they would never know. Heaven wrapped her left arm around Dieter and the mass of dough that held him. She stuck out her right arm and waved her hand wildly. "Grab me. QUICK!" Pauline came running as soon as she realized what was going on. She took Heaven's hand and yanked as hard as she could. Dieter and the dough started to tip over and the next thing Pauline knew Heaven was going down. Pauline let go. Dieter and the sticky mass he was part of fell on Heaven who landed on the floor, just twenty feet short of the dreaded guillotine cutter.

"Help, I'm suffocating," Heaven yelled. All at once everyone was on top of them. Patrick Sullivan had run out into the hall to call for help and several production workers arrived with plastic tarps and pails of water. Patrick himself grabbed Dieter around the waist and pulled him off Heaven, then tried to pull the dough out of Dieter's nose and mouth. One of the other workers started CPR, as Patrick went back in the hall and yelled for someone to call 911. Pauline helped Heaven to her feet, and one of the other bakers brought a wet towel over to wipe her face.

"Are you OK?" Patrick Sullivan asked anxiously.

"I'll be fine," Heaven said. "I just had a panic attack

with all that sticky dough everywhere. What about Dieter? Is he . . ."

"Not breathing," Patrick said tersely as the paramedics made their appearance. A plastic box was clutched tightly in Dieter's hand—the hand that Heaven hadn't grabbed a hold of. Heaven leaned down and slipped it loose, knowing that if she didn't get it before the trained professionals got there, she might not ever know what it was. She grabbed it in plain sight without any attempt to conceal her actions.

Pauline pointed at the box. "What's that?"

Heaven opened it up. A syringe fit in one side of the box, three vials of liquid were on the other. "I better give this to the medics," she said as they bent over the victim.

"Insulin," one of the men said. "He must be a diabetic. Thanks, but I don't think it will make a difference now."

Out of habit, Heaven looked around to see where Walter Jinks was. She saw him bending over the other side of the still body of Dieter Bishop. Right beside him was Ernest Powell, on his knees, praying.

You've got to be kidding." Detective Bonnie Weber said, shaking her head. She had arrived at Cafe Heaven a few minutes before. It was early, about 6:30 P.M., and Heaven had asked her friend, a homicide detective, to come by before the rush. Bonnie was off duty so she was drinking a beer, a Boulevard, the local favorite.

Heaven had gone home, showered, and changed after the disaster at the bread factory. Luckily, no one else was there. She would have hated to tell Iris and Hank how close she had come to the dreaded guillotine blade. Of course, she could have jumped to safety but Heaven would only admit to herself that once she grabbed Dieter and wrapped her arm around that sticky dough, she had felt trapped, just as trapped as poor Dieter had been.

"So let me get this straight," Bonnie said. "On Thursday some general jumps off the top of a grain elevator out in Kansas."

Heaven whisked olive oil into a mixing bowl in a steady, slow stream. She and Bonnie were having their little tête-à-tête in the kitchen where Heaven was helping with the final prep before another busy Saturday night. "We don't know that he jumped, Bonnie. But he definitely ended up on the ground, dead. And he was a retired general."

"And then this crack private detective team you run on the side here at Cafe Heaven found out that his body had traces of LSD which I assume you think wasn't something the general would take on his own?"

"You think right. He was the former head of mess halls for the army, very straight and very focused, to say the least. The police checked out the lift right after the accident. It worked perfectly. Tell me Bonnie, is someone guilty of murder if they give another someone drugs like LSD and then the second someone does something foolish like think they can fly or become one with the bread dough?"

Bonnie thought for a moment. "Good question, and I'll have to find out the answer. But the question isn't are they guilty, the question is can they be charged with murder? Big difference. But back up a minute. So Thursday the general, and today, the German. Today you all are having a tour of the bread plant, and one of your bread bakers goes to the john. The next time you see him, he's upside down in a thousand pounds of bread dough with a rig of insulin in his hand. Do you think this is like ol' Pigpen Hopkins, who got beaned over the head, then tossed in his barbeque sauce?"

Heaven smiled. "I don't think so. I do get caught up in the strangest food disasters, don't I? I couldn't see any wounds on Dieter. Of course he was pretty sticky when they took him away. He could have had a gunshot wound, and I don't think we would have seen it. The dough would have stopped any blood flow."

"Of course, the police were called?" Bonnie asked.

"Of course, but as of the time they took Dieter, or the body away, it seemed like a tragic accident. And I guess it still could be, but I doubt it."

"You don't think it was just that dough drunk thing, and he toppled in the bin? By the way, Heaven, this dough drunk business is bizarre. Don't tell me Pauline gets tipsy every morning?"

Heaven shook her head as she seasoned the salad dressing. "You have to be in an enclosed space with lots of dough. Now I'm not saying Dieter didn't suffer dizziness from the ethanol in the room. But he would have the sense to get out of there if he'd been, you know, in his right mind. And if he was diabetic, who knows what the LSD would do to him."

Bonnie took a swig of her beer and sighed. "So, at the very least, you want me to make sure the coroner checks for LSD. This Dieter, did he act loaded before he took off for the men's room? It takes a while for that stuff to work, as you probably know better than I."

Heaven almost complained about that assumption, then thought better of it. "He gave a speech at noon, and I didn't talk to him after that. He was excited when he made the speech, but I thought it was nervousness. We spoke briefly at the bakery. It was about two-thirty when we got there. I seem to remember that two and a half hours would be enough time to get pretty high, if it were LSD and not a combination of dough drunk and the wrong amount of insulin."

Bonnie went to the pass-through window. "Hey, Chris, Joe, somebody. Get me another beer, will ya." Soon the bartender, who had heard Bonnie, sat a full bottle on the window and Bonnie turned back to Heaven.

"So, what is going on with the bread bakers? Surely after two deaths, the ARTOS gang must be getting nervous. Are they planning to get out of Dodge, so to speak?" Bonnie asked.

"Actually, the conference will end a day early. Everyone decided to bake Dieter's breads tomorrow, from the chef he brought from Germany, and bring them to the party here tomorrow night. That will be the last event instead of the big French bread bake-off that was planned for Monday."

"Great," Bonnie Weber said. "You're having another one of those Sunday night parties for visiting chefs. Those are always a disaster. And what did you just say about baking bread from the chef he brought with him from Germany? What chef? Isn't he the chef?"

Heaven ignored the last question and responded to the insult first. "Always a disaster? We only lost one barbecue queen at that party, Bonnie. Surely your years on the homicide beat have given you more stamina than that. This should be a piece of cake, so to speak. The bakers are supplying bread and sweets. I'll do the savory stuff. It will be more like a wake for Dieter. And the "chef" in this case is also called the "mother". It's the sourdough starter."

Bonnie punched Heaven's arm with the beer bottle. "Insider names. I guess you couldn't be talked into just letting everyone go home without the memorial party, could you? I really didn't like the part where someone put a pair of poisoned rats in your van. Took a lot of planning and thought. And as you know, those are my least favorite criminals, the ones that think."

Heaven dipped a portion of penne pasta in a pot of boiling water and at the same time flipped some scallops and shrimp over in a hot sauté pan. "Once this conference is over, we won't have a chance to figure out what happened. Everyone will go back to their lives."

"Not the general or Dieter, babe," Bonnie said as she headed for the backdoor of the cafe kitchen. "I'll speak to the medical examiner's office, but we won't know anything until Monday. Try to get through tomorrow in one piece."

Just then Murray stuck his head through the pass-through. "Detective Weber, are you sneaking out the back? Heaven, Sal told me to tell you that you *can* patent plants."

"No way! That doesn't seem right, does it?" Heaven asked.

Bonnie paused on her way out the door. "Remember H, big companies don't just do research for the betterment of mankind. There has to be a way of making a buck, or they wouldn't be interested."

"Yeah," Heaven said, "I guess that's why the big chemical companies are getting into the grain business too. One of them, Monsanto or Dow, develops soybean seeds that are receptive to the herbicides and pesticides they also manufacture. They get it coming and going."

Bonnie waved as she walked out, throwing her empty beer bottle in the big trash container by the dishwashing machine. "That makes BIG BREAD look pretty tame by comparison, doesn't it."

Tame definitely wouldn't be a word to describe Cafe Heaven that night. It was busy from seven to eleven nonstop. A married couple had a knock-down-drag-out fight in the dining room, and the wife not only poured a drink on the husband but tried to break a wine bottle over his head. Murray had to stop the husband from strangling the wife. He called a girlfriend of the wife's to come pick her up.

Then a new busboy just disappeared. One minute he was on the floor, struggling to set up five tables that turned all at the same time, the next minute he had vanished. The waiters had to set their own tables, something that led to grumbling out in the alley, where everyone went to smoke cigarettes.

About eleven, Heaven was about to step out in the alley to make sure everyone was still speaking to everyone else. In the old days she would have smoked with them but she had stopped smoking about a year before. Even so, she had only smoked when she was at the restaurant. It was a food service trap. Lots of cooks and front-of-the-house people smoked as a way of socializing. Heaven had too. But one day she went out and stood in the alley where everyone smoked and drank a glass of ice water while she talked to the troops. After that she always drank water instead of smoking.

Ice water in hand, she ran into her daughter coming in the back door. "Hi, honey. I didn't know you were coming in tonight. Do you want to eat?"

Iris nodded. "I'm starved. I went to the nine o'clock movie with some of my high school buddies and before that we had drinks and nachos at one of the Mexican places down on the Boulevard, but that was hours ago. A couple of the girls are coming here to meet me. Where are you going?"

"Just out with the waiters, honey. Go have Murray get you a table, I should be able to leave the kitchen pretty soon and I'll come out and say hi to the girlfriends."

"Mom, don't let me forget to tell you about the patent stuff I found out this morning. I read more," Iris said as she slipped out the door to the dining room.

Heaven went back to the alley but the staff had actually gone in to do their jobs. She sat on a stack of wooden crates and sipped her water, alone in the dark. What was it about kids that made your heart ache, even when they were perfectly fine? Iris had just been home for maybe the last summer vacation of her life. She was an adult, a lovely, well-adjusted young woman. Still, the sense of loss was overwhelming. She doesn't need me anymore. I'm not her shelter from the storm. Why didn't I have more children? I could adopt, I suppose, if only the truly physically dependent will make me feel complete, those who need you to change their diaper and feed them. Heaven jumped up. Wait a minute. She almost had that inside the restaurant, people who depended on her. Some depended on her for their livelihood, some just for an hour or two of solace and a good meal. What was the matter with her? Iris was still her child. She would still depend on Heaven for a mother's love, no matter how old she got.

As Heaven started for the kitchen door, it opened. Walter Jinks stood there, hesitating.

"Walter, what are you doing here?"

"Oh, I'd planned to spend the rest of the weekend up here. I'm staying with friends, and they insisted on taking me to that fancy place on the next block. I just slipped down here while they were at the bar smoking cigars, the women too. I don't get this new cigar craze the country is in."

"Well, I do get a kick out of all these macho guys holding phallic objects in their mouths," Heaven said with a grin.

"Heaven, I just came down here because, well, Dieter's death really bothered me."

"Everyone of us could say the same, Walter. This bread conference will be one that the ARTOS members won't forget. I bet the next time they want to experience the heartland of America, they'll go to Chicago."

"Heaven, what do you think?"

"About?"

"About the chances of two people out of a small group of a hundred and twenty dying in two freak accidents?"

Heaven thought about telling Walter about her LSD theory but decided against it. Someone known for his activist work in the late sixties probably knew plenty about LSD. Walter would be the likely suspect once again. It all seemed a little too pat for Heaven's taste. Still, she didn't want to be the first one to mention LSD to Walter. Better let a trained law enforcement person do that, if indeed Dieter had been dosed too. "I know what you mean. Something's rotten in Denmark, like my grandad used to say. Even if the two deaths were honest accidents, something's not kosher."

Walter laughed. "Well, good, we agree about that. I can't for the life of me fit the two accidents together in any pattern."

Heaven led Walter back into the kitchen. It was steamy and the heat felt good. It was getting a little chilly outside. Heaven shivered. "Always the scientist, eh, Walter, looking for that link, that pattern that will shed light. Well, let's hope you don't find it because I would much rather the two things weren't part of some bigger picture. I'm still in shock from learning about our missing topsoil. And before you get going on that subject, I'm going to declare our worry session over. Come out front with me, and I'll buy you a shot of some wonderful tequila."

"Is it 100 percent agave spirits?"

Heaven pushed Walter through the swinging doors to

the dining room. "Of course it is, and aged at that. Tell me what you know about distilling tequila, Walter."

As Heaven and Walter talked small talk about tequila, Heaven tried very hard to study Walter realistically. Could he be the one causing all this trouble? Heaven knew she had been wrong before, but she felt so easy around him, comfortable. She would trust him to do the right thing for the world. Of course, in his mind that could include doing some very twisted things, Heaven kept reminding herself, like destroying those who didn't believe the same things he did about grains. She wondered if Walter was married. He was kind of cute in an intellectual, nerdy sort of middle-aged way. Maybe it was something as trite as physical attraction that was behind Heaven's bias toward Walter.

When they had their shots of Reposado Herradura, she raised her glass. "Here's to the topsoil, wherever it may be," she said as she sipped her liquor. This stuff was so smooth, you wanted to savor it. "Come over and say hi to my daughter. You met her on Thursday. Then you better head back down the street. Those cigars are close to butts by now."

Walter left shortly, followed by Iris's friends. Twenty minutes later, Iris and Heaven headed for 5th Street, Iris following her mother home in her rusted pickup truck. As they parked beside each other in the garage, Heaven asked, "What do you want me to do with the pickup? Sell it?"

Iris looked sternly at Heaven. "Over my dead body. Mom, I didn't say I was never coming back, just that I wasn't returning here to live after college. Don't be such a drama queen."

Heaven had to grin as they walked in the house. "Do you remember how excited we were when we found that truck, parked on someone's farmyard with a "For Sale" sign stuck on it?"

Iris nodded. "It was near Strong City and it cost $700. I remember we had to borrow $300 from Uncle Del. We were poor that year."

Heaven stopped at the wine rack and grabbed a bottle. "I think we need a glass of red wine to end the evening. This Truchard Syrah should do the trick. Yes, we were poor that year, but I didn't want to ask your Dad for the money. I wanted to buy you that perfectly rusted Ford myself. I paid Del back $50 a month. Who knew it would outlast several other vehicles that have lived in this garage."

"Well, I don't ever want to get rid of the truck, Mom. Why don't you drive it for a while? Hank, thinks you need a break from the van. Speaking of Hank, is he coming home soon?" Iris grabbed two wine glasses. "Should I get a glass for him?"

Heaven went up the stairs at a gallop. "No," she called back. "He'll be at the hospital all night. Let's get our jammies on."

Heaven and Iris got into their favorite sleeping tee shirts, Heaven's from the Aspen food festival she had attended in June, and Iris's from the latest Rolling Stones tour. They jumped into Heaven's bed with the wine. "I've got news for you," Heaven said, "and I'm sure it's going to upset you. This afternoon, when we were at the bread factory, Dieter died. Now, I'll tell you everything about Dieter, but then you have to tell me about the patent stuff."

"As if any patent stuff was important after that announcement. Mom, this is too weird. What happened?"

And so Heaven told her. When she was done, Iris grabbed her mother's hand. "Mom, I mean it. When I go back next week you have to promise me you'll leave all this bread stuff alone. Someone is nuts."

Heaven kissed her daughter's cheek. "So what did you learn about patents, young lady?"

"You're ignoring me but I'll keep reminding you to butt out. In the meantime, I read some more in your law book. Didn't you say BIG BREAD had applied for a patent for what the general and his staff had developed?"

"Yep," Heaven answered.

"According to that book, only the inventors can apply for a patent. If an inventor is dead, their legal representatives or guardian can apply. If one person had the idea and the other financed its development, only the person with the idea can apply," Iris recited.

"If the general developed it and BIG BREAD financed it, then BIG BREAD couldn't apply for a patent? Surely the BIG BREAD lawyers know that," Heaven said.

"Nothing ventured, nothing gained," Iris said. "I'm sure it won't be the first time an unscrupulous company ended up with a patent they didn't really deserve."

"You sound very worldly, little girl. Don't tell me the bad guy might win."

Iris jumped out of bed and blew her mother a kiss. "Call me anytime for a reality check, Mom. I'll straighten you out."

"Sleep tight. Don't let the bed bugs bite."

Iris stuck her head back in her Mom's room. "That used to scare the shit out of me when I was little. Bed bugs. Gross."

Vegetable Root Bake

1 lb. each turnips, parsnips, sweet potatoes, new potatoes.
  Other options are 'Granny Smith' apples, rutabagas,
  butternut squash, acorn squash.
Apple cider
Heavy cream
Parmesan cheese
Kosher salt and white pepper

Slice the root vegetables and layer them in a non-stick
sprayed casserole with the apples somewhere in the middle.
Season with salt and pepper on each layer and cover roots
with apple cider. Cover with foil and bake for 60 minutes at
350 degrees. Remove from the oven, uncover and add
enough heavy cream to cover the vegetables. Sprinkle with
grated Parmesan cheese and cook to tender, uncovered,
about 30 more minutes.

Twelve

It was early morning. Heaven tried to stay in bed and wait for Hank to get home from the hospital, but she was too full of energy to stay still. She was going through her dirty clothes, throwing the ones she had already examined on the floor when Hank came up the stairs.

"What are you doing, H?" Hank said as he lay face down on the bed, clothes on.

"Looking for that photo that I, that someone gave me from the bakers' tour on Thursday," Heaven said, her head down in the clothes hamper.

"That reminds me, I looked up all your dead-tissue causes. They're down in the car, honey. I forgot them. We had a hell of a night. One of the kids from down here, a Viet kid that I've known since I was five, came in with his wife in premature labor. They lost the baby. We had two gunshot wounds last night too. Lost one of them." Hank had rolled over and was in the process of taking his clothes off without getting up.

Heaven stopped tearing the house apart. She sat down

on the edge of the bed and looked at Hank. "How horrible. A friend loses his baby. I don't see how you can work in ER, honey. All that grief."

"I don't see it like that. I see all the people we help. Honey, would you pull off my shoes?" Hanks long legs were dangling off the bed. Heaven knelt down and kissed his knees as she untied his shoelaces.

"I was thinking about having a baby today," Heaven said. "Actually it was yesterday I started thinking about it. I mean, I know we could never have one of our own. I had my tubes tied years ago. But we could adopt. Of course it wouldn't be like you having your own child."

"I don't want children, H. You know that."

"Hank, another war isn't going to break out here in America next week like it did in Vietnam when you were little. You'd be such a great Dad."

"You mean like my Dad was? He tried to do the best for us. He took care of his family by working for the U.S. Army. And that's what killed him when the north came. I've grown up without a Dad. I don't want that for anyone else, so the best way to avoid heartache is no children. You had Iris. That's enough for us."

Heaven pulled off Hank's shoes and socks. She kissed the instep of his right foot.

"Oh my God. Don't start, H. I'm so tired, I can't even lift my legs to take off my own shoes. I still don't want kids."

"I'm not starting anything, darling. I have to jump in the shower and go to work."

"No you don't. It's Sunday."

"Tonight is the combo farewell to the ARTOS baking conference and wake for Dieter Bishop. He seems to have had a serious case of dough drunk."

Hank's eyes were closed but he immediately opened them. "What does that mean?"

"Say good night, Hank. I'll tell you everything when I see you next. When will that be?"

"I don't have to go back until Monday morning," Hank murmured as he pulled up the covers. "Heaven?"

Heaven was headed for the shower. "Yes, baby?"

"Didn't you tell me something about rye?"

"Yes, Dieter is, was, a rye bread expert. Why do you ask?"

Hank didn't answer. He was breathing evenly with a look of profound peacefulness on his face.

Heaven had to go back and kiss his forehead. "The sleep of a truly righteous man," she pronounced softly.

Then she hit the showers.

Thanks for coming with me, honey." Heaven said to Iris as they were driving to the cafe.

"Mom, I'm leaving in a couple of days. Of course I want to be with you. Besides, I started this bread baker's convention and I want to finish it and, it's more fun cooking when the place is closed."

"Yeah, those pesky old customers always get in the way when the place is open."

"Mom, you don't have to pay for this party, do you?"

"No, the host committee took some of the conference fees for this party, just as they did for the lunch at the hotel and the barbecue tour. I won't make a penny, but I won't go in the hole for a change."

"Well, that's something. What are we fixing?"

"I thought we'd do a country, harvest kind of thing. They had a Mennonite feast on Thursday, barbeque on Friday, a hotel lunch on Saturday, I thought fried chicken was the only thing left. I remember my grandmother talking about cooking for thrashers."

"Thrashers?"

"In the old days, everyone didn't own their own combines to harvest the wheat. A farm would hire the company that owned the machines, first horse-drawn, then later, gas combines. They would supply the hired help as well. Thrashers were hired hands that went down the Great Plains, from Minnesota to Texas, working to get the wheat harvested. I have photographs, they used to harvest with big teams of horses that pulled the combines in your great-granddad's time. Grammy used to tell me all the stories. The women would go from farm to farm and help cook for the thrashers. Supposedly the thrashers could eat more than anybody."

"And they made fried chicken?"

"Yes, and loads of fresh vegetables and mashed potatoes and pies. And they set up long tables out in the yard, like we ate lunch at Ernest Powell's."

"Have we seen Ernest Powell lately, Mom?"

"Ernest gave his big plea to the bakers for bread machines for the poor yesterday at the luncheon."

"They didn't laugh at him, did they?"

"They positively embraced the idea. ARTOS has started a foundation to buy and give bread machines to needy families all over the country. I was wrong about them being too snooty to accept a bread machine for any reason."

"I think most of the bakers seemed like nice enough folks, even if they're famous. I knew they'd come around to help ol' Ernest, who deserves some credit. Those Kansas farmers are a tricky lot. They act dumb, but they could run the country better than the politicians."

Heaven wheeled into her parking spot behind the restaurant. "Good old Kansas common sense. It must have skipped a generation, from your granddad, straight to you."

Iris smiled and hugged her Mom's arm. "We don't have to make pies for one hundred, do we?"

"No, the ARTOS gang is out at Hearth and Home Bakery baking Dieter's last rye sourdough bread and they're going to make an apple crisp or cobbler or something. And Robbie, the day dishwasher, is a great chicken fryer. He's coming in at noon," Heaven said as she unlocked the backdoor of the cafe and disarmed the alarm.

Heaven and Iris made a pot of coffee and a prep list. She had just finalized the menu the day before. September was a transition month for Kansas City in terms of vegetables. The root vegetables were just starting to be harvested and the tail end of the summer produce, like tomatoes and zucchini, were on and off. Max Mossman, her organic produce man, had arrived with plenty of green tomatoes and only a few zucchini, lots of cucumbers, the last of the corn that Heaven made into corn chow-chow the day before, and some great looking potatoes and squash. With a sigh of satisfaction, Heaven put the menu and prep list on a clipboard that she hung on a nail near the worktable. Heaven hated to start cooking until she had a prep list. If you couldn't cross something off the prep list there wasn't any sense in doing it.

ARTOS Sunday Supper Menu

Fried chicken
Meat loaf
Mashed potatoes and gravy
Root bake of turnips, parsnips, sweet potatoes, celery root
and carrots

Black-eyed peas
Collard and mustard greens
Sweet and sour red cabbage and apples
Fried green tomatoes
Marinated cucumbers and onions
Corn chow-chow
Watermelon pickles
Tomato preserves
Bread and cobbler from the bakers

"This seems like lots of items to whip out, Mom," Iris said doubtfully.

"Yes, but it's all pot food. Nothing except the chicken needs constant attention. And only the fried green tomatoes need attention at the last minute. We're not going to have appetizers. It's not the farm way. When the bakers get here, around six-thirty, we'll give them time for a drink, then put all the food out and we're done with them. I can hardly wait."

"Speaking of the farm way, what drinks go with this menu, lemonade and iced tea?"

Heaven smiled. "That is what your grandmother would have served, that's for sure. And we will have big pitchers of milk and tea, both sweetened and unsweetened. I told the bartenders last night to squeeze a lot of lemons for me. I thought we'd have something that involves gin and lemonade, maybe frozen into slushes. And beer, and although I know wine was never a part of a thrashers' supper, I have to have it. I got Rosemount Shiraz for the red and Cakebread Sauvignon Blanc for the white. We'll put the drinks we're offering on the bar in big pitchers and tubs. I don't want anyone to think they can just pick from behind the bar. ARTOS can't afford all the booze this crew could drink. If they're like most chefs, they can pack it away."

"Is anyone else coming to help?"

"Don't worry. We don't have to do it all. As I said before, Robbie will be here at noon. He'll do the chicken and stay to do the dishes later. Four front-of-the-house people will be in, a bartender, Joe and Chris. And Murray will be here late in the afternoon, to meet and greet."

"Mom, I bet you miss Sam, don't you?"

Sam was a young man who had started working at Cafe Heaven as a busboy when he was in high school. He grew up in the restaurant. Although he hadn't wanted to go to college initially, Heaven had talked him into giving it a try. First, he had gone to the junior college in Kansas City and continued to work at the restaurant. Sam had always been a great draftsman, and finally decided to take the plunge and become an architect. He had gone to New York last year to attend Cooper Union and because of his schedule, hadn't been able to come home for the summer. "Of course, I miss him terribly. He was here the first day this place opened. He and Murray. I know I must be happy for Murray, that he's started writing again, but I'm afraid he'll get famous and leave too."

Iris was busy peeling parsnips for the root bake. "Poor Mom. Your favorite waiter grows up and goes to college, your maitre d' goes back to journalism, and your daughter tells you she won't be moving back to Kansas City."

Heaven threw a potato peel across the room in the direction of her daughter. "I refuse to feel sorry for myself until I put you on the plane. I'm thrilled for Sam. And for Murray. And as for you, I know whatever you do next, you will be a huge success."

"Whoa, what happened to you overnight? When we went

home last night you were a big baby, ready to sell my poor pickup the minute I went back to school. Today you sound positively rational."

"It happens once in a while. Now I think I'll make my Mom's famous meat loaf recipe. The meatloaves don't have to go in the oven until four or five but I'll make the mixture now and get that out of the way. It's such a messy job."

"Raw ground beef and eggs and stuff? Yeah, and I know you mix it up with your hands."

Heaven pointed to a box up on the shelf. "Now, I try to remember to use the handy, dandy rubber gloves on the messy jobs. Health, food safety, bacteria under the finger-nails, you know."

"Stop. I don't want to think about gross stuff like that. Do I have to wear those rubber gloves?"

"No, we don't wear them for normal chores. It's much better to use bleach water and wash every surface down as you go. That kills the bugs better than anything." Heaven pointed at a plastic container on the counter. "I just auto-matically fill up a container with hot water and bleach when I come in the door. I did it as soon as we got done with the prep list. Try to get in the habit of washing your table and knives with bleach water and do it when you get back to England. You'll have fewer colds."

Iris rolled her eyes. "I have never known you to be a germ freak. But I'll take your suggestion, thank you very much. Should I peel the turnips next?"

At three in the afternoon, the kitchen was full of good smells, chiefly that of the fried chicken. Robbie Lunstrum had two deep hotel pans full of crispy cooked chicken parts, covered with foil and sitting on top of the big twelve-burner stove. He had two more pans of raw chicken marinating in buttermilk and two huge cast iron skillets full and crackling with chicken and his cooking solution, which Heaven suspected was a combination of cooking oil and lard. She tried never to look over when Robbie was loading his skillets. That way when people asked, she could honestly say she didn't know if lard was involved. Heaven was afraid you couldn't get such good tasting chicken without using lard.

The root bake was in big pans too, layered like escalloped potatoes only better. Red cabbage and apples were simmering, greens were in a big pot with a ham hock thrown in for good measure, black-eyed peas were almost done, beer batter was ready for the slices of green tomatoes to be dipped in and then fried.

Heaven had sliced the cucumbers and onions, added sugar, white vinegar, water and just a little Louisiana hot sauce, and put them in the walk-in cooler to cure for a few hours. Every time she made cucumber salad like that, she thought of her mother and the big garden they always had on the farm.

At the time, it had been something to gripe about when it was her turn to pull weeds. But through the years of her childhood she had come to look forward to the first salad of baby leaf lettuce in the spring, and everything that followed from that patch of earth in the backyard next to the kitchen. As each vegetable and herb sprang from the earth and flourished, it had a moment of glory at their table. Tomatoes, peppers, all varieties of beans, greens, chilies, and beautiful herbs were prepared and served in all kinds of ways. The family worked on the plans for the plot together each year, trying new things as well as the top ten favorites. There was a famous family feud over which tomato varieties to plant. The O'Malley's grew eggplants before eggplants were cool. One of their neighbors had taught them the ancient Indian way of growing corn, beans and squash together. The corn stalks became a place for the bean vines to wind around, stretching up to the sun. The squash crawled along the ground in the shade of the other two.

Even though Heaven never gave it a thought when she was growing up, the current trend in cuisine that emphasized the regional and the seasonal was just how she had been taught to cook. Canning was another part of her childhood. She had been flooded with good canning memories in August when she'd made tomato preserves and put up pickles made with watermelon and cantaloupe rind. Tonight, they would have those and the corn relish she had whipped together the day before. In the Kansas before refrigeration, farm families preserved all the garden bounty so they could eat through the winter, and those habits remained. Heaven was glad she had learned to can.

"Heaven, come out and look at the dining room," Chris and Joe called, almost at the same time. They had come in an hour before to set the tables. Iris had wandered off to help them.

For two young men who had never been on a farm, they did a good job of faking it. The dining room looked like an uptown version of the tables at Ernest Powell's. Arranging the four top tables into long continuous rows, they had covered them with white tablecloths, and over that, vintage tablecloths from the forties printed with fruits and flowers from Heaven's private tablecloth collection. Down the middle of the tables stood artful bunches of wheat tied with gold ribbon into mini-sheaves.

"Love the wheat, guys," Heaven said.

Iris was busy tying a ribbon. "Look, Mom. I just did a Martha Stewart thing."

"I won't hold it against you, honey. Now will you three start on the bar? Enough of this gracious living shit."

Chris and Joe were undaunted. "You like it and you know it, boss. What time is it?"

A voice floated into the room from the kitchen door. "Almost four I think. Of course it's almost four somewhere in the universe every moment."

This statement made Heaven and Joe and Chris and Iris all stop and stare. It came from Pauline, not usually known for her New Age proclamations. Heaven rushed over to help Pauline with the very many loaves of bread she had in her arms. Pauline had a very strange glimmer in her eyes, almost a sheen of yellowish light. She was sweating, which surprised Heaven. Pauline worked in the heat all the time and didn't sweat like this. Heaven bet the bakers had been drinking a little wine as they worked.

"So, Pauline," she said, "how's it going? These loaves look great."

Pauline smiled beatifically at the group. "And they taste good too. We ate the first fournee for lunch," she explained as she arranged the loaves down the middle of the tables. "There are more. I have to go back and pick up the rest of the bread and the dessert. But I just had to share with you."

"And what, pray tell, is fournee?" Chris asked cryptically. "Something with alcohol I bet."

Iris was the most fluent French speaker. "It means baking. Have you been having a good time today, Pauline?" she asked cautiously.

"The best," Pauline answered airily. Then Pauline's behavior became even stranger. Each time she came to a wheat centerpiece on a table, she very delicately picked it up and tossed it on the floor, and replaced it with a loaf of bread. Everyone was so astonished by this behavior that she trashed three wheat arrangements before Heaven rushed to her side.

"Pauline, I think you've had a little too much . . ."

"Champagne," Pauline said with a giggle as she grabbed a few wheat stalks out of the next grouping and started tossing them, one by one, in the air.

Heaven grabbed the remaining stalks out of her hands. "Why don't we do this? Why don't we go together over to the bakery to pick up the rest of the bread and the dessert? Doesn't that sound like fun?"

Iris and the guys, alarmed to see the ever-practical Pauline turn into a wood nymph throwing natural materials around, reacted favorably to Heaven's suggestion.

"Don't worry, Mom, we'll be fine," Iris said. "You go with Pauline. As soon as Murray or the bartender comes, I'll go back in the kitchen and check the prep list."

Heaven gently pushed Pauline toward the back door as she looked over her shoulder at the other three. Pauline was singing that old rock chestnut "Louie, Louie" at the top of her lungs, dancing as well. "Make some coffee," Heaven said. "We'll be right back."

Mrs. O'Malley's Meatloaf

4 eggs
3 lbs. ground chuck
1 10 oz. can tomato puree
1 ½ cups fine bread crumbs
2 packages dry onion soup mix
1 16 oz. bottle creamy Italian dressing
¼ cup mustard, either Dijon or coarse ground or yellow,
    then another ¼ cup to finish
1 tsp. each kosher salt and white ground pepper
1 T. each soy sauce and Worcestershire sauce

Mix all ingredients together, using ⅔ cup of the dressing.
Form into two loaves and mark them with crisscross marks
with a sharp knife. Bake on baking sheets at 350 degrees for
an hour.

Make a glaze with the remaining Italian dressing and
the second ¼ cup mustard. Pour over the meat loaves and
return to the oven for another fifteen minutes.

Thirteen

The Hearth and Home bakery was almost deserted when Heaven and Pauline arrived. This surprised Heaven.

"Where is everyone?" she asked. There were two bakery employees with white, brimless baking caps on, obviously the vanguard for the night shift, looking over the clipboards that Heaven assumed were their work orders for the night. Other than that, it was quiet.

"When I left for the cafe, everyone left to go to the hotel and change clothes. We'll meet at the restaurant," Pauline said. She had been subdued in the van. Now she looked pale, her eyes still glazed. "I don't feel good. I'm going to the bathroom," she mumbled and ran hurriedly in that direction.

Heaven chuckled. "You'll feel better if you just go ahead and throw up. It'll give you a new start," she called after her.

Heaven walked over to the worktable where twenty or so loaves of bread in assorted shapes were resting, sitting next to three big hotel pans of something with a crust over the top. Heaven, using her usual technique, carefully pinched off a chunk of crust and peeked in. She fished out a slice of apple and popped it in her mouth, then replaced the bit of crust. "Um. Local 'Jonathan' apples I bet." She automatically started putting clear plastic film over the cobblers so they could be transported. She smiled as she worked, thinking about Pauline, usually so sedate, getting drunk in the afternoon.

Then Pauline screamed, loud and long. Heaven rushed toward the scream, looking around for the bakery workers who were now nowhere to be seen. Heaven could have kicked herself. She should have checked them out immediately. Maybe they weren't really bakery workers at all. Maybe they had done something terrible to Pauline. Maybe they were robbing the place. Maybe . . .

Heaven found Pauline outside the bathroom door, staring at the floor. There, the bakery cat was having a fit. The pretty calico jumped like an electric shock had been passed through her body, then went into convulsions. "It was rolling around on the floor, screaming, and I tried to pick it up." Pauline showed Heaven the underside of her left arm. There was a vicious scratch with blood oozing from it.

Heaven put her arm around Pauline. "You poor baby. We'll take care of that when we get back to the cafe."

The cat was meowing loudly now, and writhing in what Heaven guessed was extreme pain. She wondered if it had got into the mouse poison that she assumed was around the bakery somewhere. Suddenly the cat ran up the wall, or as far up the wall as it could get. Hair standing on end, it fell on its back with a yelp, then clawed up the wall again. Heaven and Pauline watched in helpless fascination. Suddenly Pauline burst into hysterical tears.

Heaven was losing control of the situation. She was concerned about the cat of course, who was banging its head against the wall, literally. She certainly wasn't going to do the same. And trying to pick it up, like Pauline had, was out of the question. They had a party to put on.

"Pauline, let's go find those two guys that work here and tell them their kitty is loco. Stop crying right this second. How's your tummy?"

"Upset," Pauline blubbered.

The cat, in one last burst of energy, chased its tail for a few seconds, then collapsed in a convulsive heap.

"Is it dead?" Pauline looked fearfully at Heaven, as if she were afraid she would be the next one to climb the walls.

Heaven firmly turned Pauline in the other direction. "Not quite yet. We've got to get out of here. Come on now, please pull yourself together. You were so happy at the cafe. I can tell you're not used to drinking during the day."

Pauline clung to Heaven's arm pitifully. "Dieter is dead," she cried. "The guy was sweet to me, we hung out so much this weekend, I just can't get over it. What do you think happened, H?

"I think we'll know more after the medical examiner does all the tests. Bonnie is going to keep tabs on all that for us. Now, let's go find those dough boys. Can you carry a big bag of bread?"

Once Heaven and Pauline got back to the restaurant, Pauline seemed to rally. She went to the bathroom often but other than that, was calm. The cafe looked great, the crew had repaired the damage Pauline did to the centerpieces and had set up the bar. Some of the ARTOS folks were already arriving. To the man, they had the same giddy energy that Pauline had exhibited earlier. Of course, they had been through some harrowing experiences since coming to Kansas City. It was no wonder they had had a drunken time at the bakery today. They were all probably eager to leave town, get back to their own businesses and write their stories for *Food and Wine* magazine, or whatever. Heaven shuddered at the thought of how this conference would look in print.

"Heaven, can I ask you a favor?"

It was Patrick Sullivan. He was shaking. His light blue polo shirt had big sweat marks in the middle of his chest. His face was coated with a sheen of sweat and his hair was mussed.

"Patrick, what in the hell . . . What's the matter?"

Patrick didn't seem to realize how rough he looked. He just blinked. "Nothing. I just wonder if you could turn up the heat. I'm freezing."

"You're freezing, and you're covered with sweat. You must be coming down with something. I'll turn on the heat, but it was in the high fifties today, perfect September weather."

Patrick looked at her as if she had questioned his parentage. "It's not just me," he snapped. "Everyone is cold. I just decided to do something about it."

Heaven eyed him as she moved toward the thermostat. "Don't take that turn with me, young man. I know this has been a rough time for you, Patrick, and I'm sorry. I'm sorry you compromised your principals by going to work for BIG BREAD. I'm sorry they made you their patsy at this artisan bread conference. I'm very sorry that Dieter Bishop was found dead in the dough in your proofing room. Now let's just try to remain civil for two more hours, and then this unpleasantness will be behind us, OK?"

Patrick looked as though he was going to burst into tears. "I'm sorry, Heaven. Since I moved to Kansas City I've been wanting to meet you, maybe be friends. Now I've messed it up. I don't know if I can make it two more hours."

"Oh, buck up. If you can sell that air-filled, chemical-filled shit you call bread, you can hold yourself together two more hours. Jesus, what did you guys drink today? Pauline was a mess too."

"Just some bottles of wine with lunch. Something from the Rhone, I think. And some Möet Chandon that Gail Gand from Chicago brought. She's real nice. Everyone is wound up, what with the general and Dieter. It was relaxing to get back in a real bakery and do what we do best, bake bread. Or rather what they do best."

Heaven cut in quickly. "Don't start feeling sorry for yourself again. Just answer a couple of questions. Was Walter Jinks at the bakery today?"

"Yeah, he was there. Ernest Powell too. But Ernest left around noon. Said he had to get home in time to do the chores. His wife and neighbors had been covering for him."

"I don't see Walter," Heaven said as she scanned the room.

Patrick lurched towards the crowd, unsteady on his feet. Heaven was almost sorry she had read him out. "I'm sure he'll be here," Patrick said. "He did an experiment."

Heaven didn't like the sound of that. "What kind of experiment?"

"He and one of the bakers, I can't remember which, baked some bread out of his grain mixture."

"Mixtures like the ones we had at his farm?"

"He said these were made out of a special mix. They had been working on it night and day, he said. He wanted to surprise us. It's a secret."

"What's a secret?" Heaven asked.

"Which loaves are made out of the regular wheat flour and which are made out of the special Walter mixture. He's sure no one will be able to tell."

"It must be a hell of a lot better than the stuff we had Thursday. Well, that will give the bread experts something to do tonight. Patrick, just remain calm," Heaven said as she headed for the kitchen.

"Wait," Patrick shrieked. The crowd turned toward them and Heaven returned to his side.

"Wait, what?" Heaven snapped. "What is your problem? And keep your voice down."

Patrick tried a stage whisper. He cupped his hand around his mouth. "I'm so sorry about the rats. I didn't know you were terrified of rats, I just wanted . . ."

Heaven jerked Patrick's arm and pulled him close. She didn't want him yapping about rats and getting everyone all whipped up. "What are you saying?"

"I thought if I did something that would make people sorry for BIG BREAD, like we were being threatened, . . ." Patrick lurched into a chair. "And everyone knows who you are so I thought. . . ." His head hit the table and he moaned. "I don't feel good."

Heaven leaned down and picked up Patrick Sullivan's lolling head by the hair, removing his glasses and putting them on the table.

"I need my glasses," Patrick said fearfully.

Heaven leaned down near his ear to talk. "Okay, now, listen to me. Don't start spilling your guts about your stupid rat stunt. These people will be gone tomorrow and they don't have to know you're the jerk who played a lousy sympathy scam. I'll deal with you later. Now, put your addled brain on rest for a minute," Heaven said as she let go of

Patrick's hair and his head fell down on the table. "Yes, ma'am," his muffled voice said pitifully.

Heaven was furious with Patrick but also relieved that one part of the puzzle was cleared up. At this point, Heaven had to concentrate on feeding the ARTOS crowd and getting them out of there. She slipped back in the kitchen where Iris was busy, frying the batter-dipped green tomato slices. She looked up and smiled at her mother. "So, how's Pauline?"

"I think she might be having the first daylight hangover of her life. She's calmed down. People are arriving. Why don't you go out and help Murray play hostess. You know who everyone is, and he doesn't."

Iris quickly took her apron off. "Gladly. It's hot over this grease."

Heaven tilted a big pot of greens sideways and spooned them out in a huge crock bowl. She looked up as Iris headed out to the front. "Thanks for helping today. We didn't even eat lunch. Are you hungry?"

Iris smiled back at Heaven. "I made a sandwich with some of Dieter's sourdough while you were gone and I had a piece of fried chicken. I'm glad I'm here for the denouement. I want to see this ARTOS conference to the bitter end. But I also want a beer, bad. I'm off to the bar."

Out in the dining room, Robbie Lunstrum, dishwasher and chicken fryer extraordinare was blushing. Heaven had insisted he put on a clean apron and come out in the dining room to accept kudos. The bakers had been blown away by the whole meal, but the chicken had definitely been the hit. Heaven refused to take credit for Robbie's good work.

He stood by the end of the food table, ducking his head when someone gushed over his crispy crust. Heaven overheard him being vague about what he fried in. Maybe chef's pride made every cook keep their secrets, or maybe Robbie sensed this group might freak if they heard the word lard.

While Robbie was out front, Heaven handled the dishwashing machine. She didn't want to stay here a minute longer than necessary. If she let the dishes pile up, Robbie would be here till midnight. That meant she would too, so she loaded dirty dishes cheerfully, thinking of what she would do to Patrick Sullivan to get even.

All of a sudden, Murray pushed open the swinging doors to the kitchen and stuck his head in. "Hey, Boss," he said with worry in his voice. "You better come out here."

"Because?"

"Because something's very wrong. People are starting to get stomach pains. And chills. And I think they're all drunk as skunks, is what I think. Did we give 'um some bad chicken?"

Heaven gestured for Murray until he stepped all the way into the kitchen. Then she frowned and started scolding him. "Don't joke about that kind of shit. For your information, food poisoning is very rare, and food-borne illness takes time to develop. If they're getting sick, it's definitely not from the chicken. Quick, go get Robbie. I don't want anyone to accuse him. I'm where the buck stops."

Murray disappeared and came back with Robbie. "As you know, Heaven, I'm an expert on drunkenness," Robbie said with good humor. "And I think we've got a roomful with a snoot full." Robbie was a sixty-something alcoholic who had been sober for enough years to talk with authority about both sides of the picture.

216

"Robbie, no one said anything about the chicken making them sick, did they?"

"No, Heaven, that would require higher reasoning. I'm glad to have been a part of this night, no matter how many hangovers occur tomorrow. Now I see what a pleasure it is to cook for those that appreciate it. I'll go back to my dish machine now," Robbie said with his usual dignity.

Heaven kissed him on the cheek. "You the man, Robbie." Then, taking a deep breath, she followed Murray out into the hot air of the dining room.

The scene reminded her of Hieronymus Bosch's paintings, some netherworld of lost souls.

Heaven didn't know where to start. How many things were wrong with this picture? She took Murray's hand and they walked the room together.

"Oh, God, I'm so cold," Patrick Sullivan mumbled. He looked worse than before, elbows on the table with his hands holding up his head. He looked pleadingly at Heaven. "I think our lunch must have made us sick. You look OK, and you weren't there. I've thrown up twice in the last thirty minutes."

Heaven quickly went behind the bar and put ice in a bar towel. She gave the ice pack to Patrick. "Put that on the back of your neck for right now. What did you guys have for lunch anyway?"

"One of the chefs made a big batch of white veal stew while we were working the sourdough. Nothing special, no weird ingredients."

Heaven moved on. Next were two bakers from Chicago writhing on the floor. Next to them and totally ignoring them were a dozen people engaged in animated conversation, eyes shining with religious zeal as they discussed various flour mills. The way they were "rapping," Heaven would have sworn they were on cocaine. She looked closely at the eyes of the talkers. She found the opposite of what she had expected, instead of pinpoint pupils, their pupils were huge.

Heaven looked around for Pauline and finally found her sitting on the floor in the corner of the dining room. "Pauline, what are you doing, honey?" Heaven said gently as she knelt beside her friend.

Pauline closed her eyes for a moment and then looked up at Heaven with terror in her eyes. "Room spinning. And it got bigger. Room was too big. Everybody was laughing at me, and they made the room go too fast."

Suddenly there was a crash of dishes. A tiny woman, a bakery owner from Aspen, had pulled one of the vintage tablecloths off the table, sending dirty plates and wine glasses everywhere. Some of the bakers around her laughed maniacally, others didn't even seem to notice what she'd done. Swirling the tablecloth above her head she yelled, "All these flowers! Aren't they beautiful? Look how fast they're growing. Aren't these the most beautiful flowers?" Suddenly she was rolling on the floor, the tablecloth wrapped around her like a shroud.

Chris and Joe and the rest of the staff had been trying to help those that were sick to their stomachs make it to the bathroom, but the smell of vomit was strong. Robbie had come out of the kitchen when he heard the sound of broken dishes. "Maybe I was wrong. They don't seem drunk anymore. Did my chicken . . . "

"Of course not," Heaven assured him. "It must have been something from breakfast, possibly dinner last night. Actually, I don't think it's food poisoning at all. Murray, when did this situation get out of hand? How come you didn't tell me sooner?"

"Heaven, I swear. One minute the whole crowd was having a ball, the next it was 1967 all over again."

Joe and Chris backed up Murray's version of events. "You're right, Murray," Chris said. "If I didn't know better, I'd think they were tripping."

Murray and Heaven, thinking of the general, gave each other meaningful looks.

"Heaven, I think you should call Hank," Joe said soberly. "Whatever is making these people sick is making their sweat smell terrible, like dead mice kinda. It must be something bad. I don't know how much longer we can be of any help."

Heaven looked around the room. It was like a B movie version of an insane asylum. One of the bakers from Los Angeles was tearing the shirt right off his body, weeping as he did so. People were on the floor, some curled up in a fetal position, some crawling around on all fours. The talkers were still at it.

Heaven stepped over to the phone on the bar and called home. "Hank, I'm sorry to wake you but we've got a situation here. This whole group of bakers has gone nuts on us, and they're sick to boot."

Hank's voice sounded tense when he responded. "How are they sick?"

"Throwing up, chills, some of them act like they just snorted a gram of cocaine, some of them seem paranoid. I think some might be hallucinating."

"Heaven, I think I know what's the matter with them. I'll be right there but then we'll have to call the hospital for help. You might want to call your police friend."

"Bonnie? I'd ask you why but that would take too long. Just hurry, please." The phone was dead before Heaven could say good-bye.

Murray had been making ice packs as Heaven talked to Hank, Chris and Joe had been passing them out. All of a sudden Chris started, as if he had suddenly remembered something. "Heaven, where's Iris?"

Heaven felt like she had been struck by lightning. How could she have overlooked her own daughter, or her daughter's absence? Frantically she ran to the kitchen. Maybe Iris had gone back to help Robbie and hadn't come out to see what the commotion was about. She wasn't there. Quickly Heaven checked the bathroom. Two women from Florida were being sick in the two stalls. They started pleading for assistance but Heaven didn't even stop to reassure them. She wheeled around the room, spotted Pauline still crouched in her corner and made a beeline for her.

"Pauline, have you seen Iris?"

"No, just these wonderful sunflowers," Pauline babbled. "See how tall they've grown? No iris, no roses, just sunflowers." She pointed up at the ceiling.

Heaven wanted to shake her but she knew that a little motherly shake wasn't going to straighten Pauline out, or anyone else in the room for that matter. She headed back to the phone. As she dialed Detective Bonnie Weber's home phone number she spotted Iris running down the sidewalk on the other side of 39th Street, next to Sal's. Her heart leaped. She knew she needed to get Bonnie over here so she yelled, "Somebody help please. Joe, Chris, Murray. Iris is across the street. Someone go get her."

Joe and Chris headed out the door, and Bonnie Weber answered her phone. "This had better be good," she said in lieu of hello.

"Bonnie, it's Heaven. We've got a serious problem over here at the restaurant."

"Who's dead?" Bonnie asked tersely.

"No one yet but the entire group of bread bakers has gone bonkers. I think they've been poisoned. I called Hank and . . ."

"I'm on my way," Bonnie said and hung up.

Iris. Heaven couldn't wait. She went outside and saw the three of them, almost two blocks away. Iris was running as if she were at the Olympics. Neither Joe nor Chris were out of shape, but they hadn't been able to catch her. Heaven could hear them calling Iris's name. She felt fear wash over her. What if Iris ran out in front of a car? Didn't that used to happen when people took psychedelics? Just as she was ready to start the chase herself, she saw Chris grab Iris from the back and pull her to a stop. Soon Joe joined them and the three turned and headed back toward the cafe. Iris started shrieking at the top of her lungs, loud screams that pierced the Sunday evening quiet on 39th Street. Heaven started crying.

Red Cabbage and Apples

1 large head red cabbage
3 'Granny Smith' apples, sliced, but not peeled
1 cup sugar
1 cup red wine vinegar
2 T. olive oil
2 T. butter
Kosher salt and white ground pepper

Melt the butter and heat oil together in a large, heavy sauté pan. Thinly slice the cabbage and sauté over low heat. When the cabbage starts to soften, add the apples. In a separate heavy saucepan slowly melt the sugar, stirring often when the edges start to liquefy. When the sugar is completely melted and browned, add it to the cabbage. Add the vinegar and seasonings and cook until the cabbage is caramelized.

Fourteen

Bonnie Weber put down the medical book. "Well, I'll be damned. I wouldn't believe it if I didn't see it right here in front of me."

Hank looked up from the photocopied papers he was studying and smiled wanly. Cafe Heaven looked like hell. It had become an annex to the hospital. Only the two most serious victims had been admitted to the real medical center down the street, one for a messy cut from a broken wine bottle and an older man from Pittsburgh who had convulsed badly. The rest of ARTOS had been looked at by emergency room doctors who, like Hank, were off duty and had responded to their friend's request for help. Hank brought the copies of pertinent medical info he had made for Heaven earlier and had gone back and checked out several medical books from the med center library. He had also borrowed blankets and pillows from the hospital, not that they were getting much use. The bakers couldn't sleep. Chills, sickness, and hallucinations continued. Hank's friends had taken blood samples from at least half the group. They were keeping an eye on everyone until they heard from the lab and could come up with a diagnosis, then they would start treatment.

Heaven came out of the kitchen, her eyes rimmed as red as her hair from crying. "When do we hear from the lab?" she asked.

Hank glanced at his watch, got up and poured a cup of coffee and handed it to Heaven. "Soon. I know it seems like a long time but its only been two hours since you called me at home."

"How's Iris?" Murray asked.

"Better," Hank said. "I told her what we thought was wrong with her and all the rest of these poor suckers. It seemed to make her less anxious. She's trying to rest, lying down on top of the worktable. She even cracked a joke, something about now that she knew she was supposed to have fun, she'd try to. Oh, dear God," Hank murmered as he looked around the room. "How did this happen?"

Bonnie held up her hand. "Hold on. I'm still trying to understand just what it is we're dealing with here. I'm up to where the general had LSD in his system and a black tongue. Hank you did some research at the hospital and found a connection between those two things.

Hank nodded. "Ergot."

"Ergot?" Chris and Joe asked together. They had been cleaning up around the dining room. "Ergot? What's that? We weren't in on the detective work Murray did on Friday." They glared first at Murray, then Heaven, as though a sacred trust had been broken.

"Sorry, guys," Murray said. "There hasn't been any time for a session at Sal's." When they could, the whole crew liked to go over to Sal's to figure out their problems. "But I didn't find out about ergot. No, sir. Hank did."

Hank grabbed Heaven's hand and pulled her next to him. "Sit down," he said.

"No," Heaven answered. "I want to go back to Iris, but I need to know too. What is this ergot stuff?"

"A fungus," Bonnie Weber chimed in. "Some kinda fungus."

"*Claviceps purpurea,*" Hank explained. A toxic fungus that evidently parasites rye grain and can poison livestock and humans. It will affect other grasses too but it really likes rye."

"But where does the LSD come in?" Heaven asked anxiously.

Bonnie pointed at the photocopied sheet of paper lying on the table. "When you bake it, it turns into LSD."

Chris and Joe looked incredulous.

Hank pointed to the book in front of him. "No, it's true. The ergot alkaloids contain lysergic acid. That's the chemical structure right there, $C_{15}H_{15}N_2CON$, better known as lysergic acid diethylamide. Evidently one of the alkaloids, ergotamine, converts to LSD in the baking process."

"But," Murray protested, "it says the milling companies watch for ergot closely. They can test for it. How could this stuff slip by?"

Heaven's eyes narrowed. "Well, the first name that comes to mind is Walter Jinks and his damned experimental grains which I'm sure aren't tested by the government. Pauline said he slipped some of his breads into the party breads, trying to see if anyone could pick them out. And Walter never showed up here tonight. Then there's Dieter's sourdough rye. It was made from Dieter's own rye patch somewhere in Germany. I think it's safe to assume no one checked it for ergot and the bakers made twenty loaves of bread, supposedly out of that flour. If those two don't have the acid rye, then there's the Milling and Grain International Studies Laboratory in Manhattan, Kansas. They're doing all sorts of biogenetic experiments there, and the general had LSD in his system. And if that's not enough suspect grain sources, how about ol' Patrick Sullivan and his research and development for BIG BREAD. Dieter took a dive in the dough over at BIG BREAD. For all we know they grow the stuff and are plotting to take over the world with ergot, as if their regular bread wasn't bad enough."

No one said a word for a minute. When Heaven got riled up it was hard to figure how to respond safely. Hank was brave. He pulled another book to the top of the pile and spoke up. "And that's not all of the possibilities. Ergot causes vasoconstriction. In the Middle Ages midwives and physicians used it to either cause abortions by inducing contraction of the uterine muscles or to stop uterine hemorrhaging after childbirth. It's still used today to stop hemorrhage. Also another derivative is used for migraine headaches so some of it is grown commercially in Minnesota and somewhere in Europe, probably Germany, for medical purposes. It can be obtained, is what I'm trying to say."

Bonnie shook her head. "As usual, the more you know, the more confusing it gets. Vasoconstriction? Is that what causes the necrosis, the dead tissue?"

Hank nodded. "No blood circulating for a while and any tissue becomes gangrenous. That's usually manifested in the fingers and toes and the tip of the tongue, like Heaven noticed on the general."

Heaven was sick with worry. Would Iris lose her toes? "So on a good day, this stuff can cause gangrene. And then, if you bake it up in a loaf of bread, it turns into acid. Great."

Bonnie looked down at the book she'd been reading. "It

says in the Middle Ages whole villages would go nuts on this stuff. It may be what caused the Salem witch trials. Even in 1951, a village in France got dosed. Three people died and 300 were affected. Oh, and some of them thought they could fly."

"Just like the general," Murray said thoughtfully.

Another wave of fear came over Heaven. "Thank God we're on the first floor. I'm going back to Iris. Let me know when the lab calls."

Just then, the phone rang and three female bakers started fighting with each other, pulling hair and rolling on the floor in angry hysteria. Hank answered the phone, and Detective Weber and the rest of the crew went to break up the cat fight. Heaven stopped on her way to the kitchen and looked hopefully at Hank on the phone. He hung up quickly and nodded. "It's official. Lysergic acid, ergot alkaloids galore."

"What can they do?" Bonnie called from across the room, her hands full holding a buxom blonde not unlike herself.

Heaven walked over and hugged Hank, feeling that as bad as it was, maybe a solution was near. Iris appeared from the kitchen and stood by her mother, shaking and covered with sweat, eyes burning bright. Heaven took her daughter's hands.

"It's too late to pump stomachs. Everyone but Iris had the bread at lunch and Iris had her sandwich."

"Around four," Iris said calmly. "Aren't you glad you weren't hungry," she said with a hollow laugh directed at Joe and Chris.

"Yes, for once I ate before I came to work," Joe said, almost guilty he hadn't joined Iris in a snack. He turned to Hank. "Isn't there something else they can do?"

"Yes, there is. We can give everyone a vasodilator so they won't have tissue damage. And sodium nitroprusside will work for those that are experiencing hypertension." He gazed over at the talkers. "The convulsions can be treated with diazepam. Are the buses still parked in front?"

"Yes, but the bus drivers are in just as bad shape as everyone else. They had lunch at the bakery and they came wandering in babbling about tiny little purple cars that were crashing into their buses," Chris said.

"Can anyone drive a bus?" Hank asked. "We need to take everyone to the hospital for treatment."

Bonnie slipped her sweater on. "I have my chauffeur's license. I'll fill up one bus. We'll have to take the rest by car. This should be fun," she said cryptically.

Hank and Heaven stood in the hospital parking lot. It was a little after dawn and the pink light was just showing over the tops of trees to the east. It was going to be another pretty September day.

Heaven was pacing.

"Heaven, for the last time, please don't do this," Hank pleaded.

"I don't have a choice, Hank. Why can't you see that? I have to talk to Walter Jinks, to see if he did this to Iris, to everyone."

"Iris is going to be fine, and so is everyone except Mr. White from Pittsburgh."

Heaven kicked at the side of her van. "Poor Mr. White is paralyzed."

Hank shook his head. "Maybe not for long. I don't think his paralysis is permanent. If this Walter is responsible you'll be in danger. Wait and let Detective Weber go with you, or Murray. Or wait until this afternoon and I'll go with you."

Heaven shook her head vehemently. "You have to stay with Iris. I don't want her to be involved in this any more than she has . . ." Heaven's voice broke. She started again. "Bonnie had to go in to work, and she has no authority in the middle of Kansas anyway. Murray and Chris and Joe only went home to sleep an hour ago. I certainly wouldn't expect them to get up and go down the road with me. And I'm not waiting, for them or for you. Thanks for saving all the bakers. Now go back inside and let me leave. I promise one thing. I promise I'll let my brother know where I am. After all, I don't want another disaster, believe me. What about everyone in there? When will they get to leave?"

"We'll keep them until they're not hallucinating or experiencing paranoia anymore," Hank said. "Twenty-four hours at least."

Heaven pecked Hank on the cheek and opened the door of her van. "Take care of my little girl," she said, her eyes flashing with anger at the thought of what had happened to Iris. Without giving Hank a chance to say another word she started the van and pulled out onto 39th Street with a screech of tires.

"Heaven!" Hank yelled and ran out to the curb.

Heaven stopped and rolled down the window an inch or two. She was shaking her head in advance of any final argument.

"Don't speed," Hank said with a little wave. Heaven waved back and was gone.

Heaven lied. She drove too fast and she didn't let anyone know where she was. She meant to go by Del's before she went to GRIP but she was possessed. Her fury had propelled her down the highway in record time. Somehow she had avoided a speeding ticket. She knew it was foolish to not let someone out here know what she was doing, but she also knew she would have a lot of explaining to do to her brother. She just couldn't take the time to do that. She'd rip Walter's heart out, then she'd go to her brother's farm.

Of course, she wasn't at all sure Walter had planted the ergot-tainted flour. Why would he? Had he been trying to change the world for so long he'd just lost touch of reality? Had his competitors become his enemies? The bad grain from Germany, the big corporation, the rival research facility, all were still options.

Walter was just the first person Heaven could think of. So many things pointed to him. Walter had a lot riding on his version of the future of bread. He had a farm and so theoretically he could grow rye with ergot growing on it. If they could grow ergot rye for medical purposes then surely Walter could do it. He had taken a stand publicly against the Milling and Grain International Studies Laboratory and its director. He hated BIG BREAD, INC. But would he put people's lives in jeopardy for his cause? Walter thought that was precisely what depending on wheat to feed the world was doing, putting the world in jeopardy. It wouldn't be such a stretch for him to do the same to make his point.

Heaven pulled into the yard of the Grains Research Institute for Peace. Two student interns were lugging a big stalk of some plant over to the mill. They threw the plant inside the stone building and then came over to Heaven.

"Hi, I'm Heaven Lee, from Kansas City. Well, actually I grew up around here. Del O'Malley is my brother. I was here last week with the bread bakers. Something happened yesterday. I need to talk to Walter." Heaven realized she was babbling. So she shut up and looked expectantly at the two young men.

One of them shifted from foot to foot uncomfortably. "Walter was sick when he came home yesterday. He thought it was the flu. He said it hit him at some bakery, I guess all the bakers were there making bread. He came home early he said, before the party at your cafe, I guess."

Heaven could see Walter dosing himself to make the whole thing look good. Clever. "Where is he?"

The other young man spoke up. "That's what we want to know. We were here when he came home last evening. We asked him if we should stay but he said no, he wanted to go to bed, just sleep it off. So we went back into Manhattan, where we're in school. When we got here this morning, Walter wasn't around." The two young men exchanged glances. "It was pretty bad in his bedroom, he'd vomited, and I guess he was too sick to clean it up. We thought maybe he'd gone to the hospital but his truck was still here. We checked at the hospital, thought maybe he'd called an ambulance. He wasn't there either."

Heaven looked around. She imagined what Iris would have done with this much wide-open space last night. A person tripping on LSD on a big farm could be anywhere. Of course if that person knew they were going to be hallucinating, it would make more sense for him to lock himself in the house or to get help under the guise of having the flu. If Walter had been the one doing all this, surely he would have had a plan, like not eating the bad bread if he wasn't going to stay with the group. "Why don't we do this," Heaven said breezily. "Why don't I take a look around the farm and you guys do whatever you're supposed to be doing. Maybe he went for a walk. Sometimes when you have the chills and are sweating a lot, you want fresh air. Maybe he was just too sick to get back home."

"You can take the golf cart," one of the boys said. "Most of the fields have cart paths around them. Walter did that so he could take funders on the grand tour, as he called it." He led her toward a small outbuilding. In it were assorted riding lawnmowers, bicycles, a motorcycle, and two golf carts. He dropped a battery that had been charging into one of the carts and drove it over to Heaven.

"Thanks. Wish me luck," Heaven called as she lurched off. She stopped the cart and looked over her shoulder. "If for some reason I'm not back in an hour, come find me."

The two young men looked at her with surprise. She smiled. "You can see I'm not very good at driving this thing. I don't want to wipe out and be stranded on the back forty." With that little bit of insurance, Heaven took off. If it turned ugly with Walter, all she had to do was survive more than an hour and she should be rescued. Unless those boys were so brainwashed with Walter's perennial polyculture dogma that they were part of the plot. Well, she couldn't worry about that now. She had ignored all safety precautions by not telling her brother where she was and what she was doing. Those two students had to be good guys, that's all there was to it.

Half an hour later, Heaven was reasonably sure Walter wasn't walking out in an open field. She guessed he could be crouching behind some tall prairie grass, but she had checked all the fields that the ARTOS group had toured. No Walter.

"I'd probably go to the woods if I was high on acid. Commune with nature," she mumbled as she left her cart and started for a thick stand of oak trees. As she tromped into the dense foliage, the sunlight was diffused by the leaf cover.

"This is a perfect place for morels to grow—fallen oak trees, moisture. I'll have to remember this area during morel season," she told herself as she hopped over dead tree trunks and small shrubs. All of a sudden, in the middle of the trees, there were signs of civilization, of cultivated plant life. There was a definite path made of wood chips that weren't just part of the forest floor. They were the kind of wood chips that you bought at a garden supply store to make a path through your yard. Ahead she saw plants that were surrounded with chain link fencing, the kind you put around baby trees or plants so dogs wouldn't piss on them. Heaven took a deep breath. The air was filled with an unmistakable, pungent aroma.

"Want a toke?" a voice asked. It was Walter Jinks, sitting on the ground, leaning up against a tree, smoking a joint. Heaven recognized the protected plants as some of the most beautiful marihuana she had seen in years. They were tall, well over six feet, with big opulent buds with long red hairs full of resin.

"Walter, what in the hell is going on here? Are you OK?"

Walter shook his head. He looked bad, his skin had a greenish cast, and his eyes were glazed over. Heaven's heart sank. If Walter had eaten enough bread to be this sick, could he be behind this whole ergot business? If he were responsible he would know how dangerous and unpredictable the fungus was. Could he be on a suicide mission? No need for that. Dieter and the general were already dead. Remorse? A gun would be easier. Heaven walked over to the tree that was holding the slumped Walter up.

She sat down beside him and took the joint out of his hand, took a big pull off it and handed it back.

"Walter, anybody ever tell you this stuff is illegal. I used to be a lawyer. I know."

Walter tried a smile. "How do you think I financed my research all these years?"

"Well, take it from me, illegal activities can reach out and bite you in the ass when you least suspect it. But we have some serious problems without the feds, Walter. The general and I'll bet Dieter Bishop and all the bread bakers at the ARTOS convention have been eating bread that was contaminated with ergot. You do know about ergot, eh Walter?"

Walter looked down at his body as if he had just discovered it again. "Is that what this is?"

"Yes, Walter, ergot turns into LSD when the bad bread bakes. It made the general think he could fly and Dieter think he could embrace the dough, become one with it. And the whole baking conference including my only daughter is now in the hospital in Kansas City. One man is paralyzed. I am pissed, Walter. Did you do this?"

Walter was hugging himself, laughing maniacally. "I knew I'd felt like this before, but I couldn't remember when or why. That's how I knew I wasn't dying, because I'd felt like this before. Was it always this bad?"

Heaven stood up and pulled Walter to his feet. "No, as it happens this ergot trip is much stronger than the stuff we took back in the sixties. A whole village in France went down for days in the 1950s. People thought they could fly just like the good general. You and my daughter have a long, bad day ahead, baby. Now, pretend I'm the avenging angel sent from above. If you lie to me you will never get out of the terror you experienced out here by yourself in the woods last night. Or if you had a good time out here by yourself in the woods last light, then if you lie to me, you will have the worst rest of your life you can ever dream. Did you plant ergot in the flour?"

Walter tried to focus, his eyes filled with tears. "I've spent my whole life trying to save life, create a better life. I did not do this."

Heaven slung one of Walter's arms around her neck and started pulling him toward the path. "I don't know why, I guess you could still be scamming in your condition, but I believe you. I'm giving you the benefit of the truth serum coursing through your veins. We need to get you to the hospital. I know what they can do to make it better. Try to walk, damn it."

Oatmeal Cookies

The idea here is very practical and Midwestern. You make up a big batch of the cookie mix that will keep for a long time in the refrigerator, then add the eggs, the perishable ingredient, and the extras to the mix as you want to bake off cookies.

To make 2 gallons cookie mix:
3 cups white sugar
3 cups brown sugar
6 cups sifted all-purpose flour
4 tsp. kosher salt
4 tsp. baking soda
4 cups solid shortening, such as Crisco. You can use butter, but it's not the Kansas way.
12 cups rolled oats

Combine everything but the oats until thoroughly mixed. Then add the oats and mix in. This is the base that can be chilled and kept for a month.

2 eggs, beaten
2 T. vanilla
4 cups cookie mix

¾ cup of any of the following: raisins, pecans, walnuts, coconut, chocolate chips, butterscotch chips.

Combine all these ingredients, form into balls, flatten and bake. Depending on the size, it usually takes 10 minutes at 350 degrees for a medium-sized cookie.

Fifteen

Heaven put down the telephone and looked over at her brother. "I talked to her. She's feeling better, not so sick to her stomach."

Del picked up their lunch plates and shook his head. "This is some story, sis. I think that whole ARTOS bunch is lucky you'd already asked Hank about this ergot stuff."

"I didn't actually ask him about ergot. I asked him what caused necrosis, cells to die. He was the one who found out about ergot." Heaven had followed Del into the kitchen and was taking the lid off the cookie jar. Oatmeal raisin. She took two and munched into one. "Good. Are these your famous oatmeal cookies, Del?"

"Yeah," Del answered distractedly. "Hank found the ergot because you asked him. And then he and you put two and two together. If you hadn't known what's what, some of those bakers could have ended up like General Mills." Del rinsed their plates and stuck them in the dish machine. "Iris too."

"Don't you think I know that? Don't you think that's why

I drove out here like a bat outta hell this morning? I was sure Walter was the bad guy and I ended up taking him to the hospital in Manhattan, calling Hank so he could tell the doctor what to do. I saved the life of the person I drove out here to beat the hell out of."

Del grabbed a cookie and took a bite, looking thoughtfully at Heaven. "How in the heck could you prove it?"

"Prove what?"

"Prove any of it. How could a jury convict anyone of a crime on this deal? Could you honestly say for 100 percent certain that this ergot is what made the general fly off that building, or the German fella dive into that bread dough?"

"We know the general had LSD in his system and when the tests come back, Dieter will have it too," Heaven said defensively.

"And did anyone see Walter or anyone else for that matter, putting the ergot in flour that was baked into bread that those two fellas ate? The evidence is all eaten up, little sister, just like that Alfred Hitchcock show with the leg of lamb."

"I don't give a fig about proving something to a jury. I just wanted to beat the truth out of Walter, before I changed my mind and decided to save his life instead. Now, I'm just exhausted. I didn't sleep a wink and my adrenalin is gone." Heaven put her arms around her brother's neck and leaned on him.

Del patted Heaven's head. "Two things. Let this ergot thing go. You can't prove anything, and there is a chance it was just an accident of nature, like you said happened in the Middle Ages. Let the bakers get out of the hospital and go back to wherever they came from. Be thankful your daughter is going to be OK. Now, number two. Don't you dare start back to Kansas City until you rest for a couple of hours. You need to close your eyes, honey. No one wants you to have an accident on the way home."

Heaven gave her brother a big kiss. "I will, I promise. Thanks for caring."

Del looked at his watch. "I've got to go. There's a problem with the livestock. Ernest Powell has lost two of his dairy cows in the last couple of days and so have the Akers. I'm going to meet the vet over at the feed lot. I sure don't want sick cattle over there."

Heaven felt the light bulb go on but she wasn't sure why. "Thanks again, bro. By the way, where's Debbie?"

"In Salina at an estate auction," Del said as he walked out the kitchen door. "Heaven, take a nap and call me when you get to Kansas City. You don't, I'll worry."

Heaven tried to lie down on the couch and rest, but her mind was racing. She remembered. "The cows," Heaven yelped. Ernest's cows. Cattle are affected by ergot. They die. Ernest's neighbors' cows died too. The neighbors' son runs into a train. Bingo. Heaven grabbed her keys and ran out the door.

Heaven kicked up gravel as she wheeled into the driveway at Ernest Powell's farm. She saw Mrs. Powell, attractive in that modest Mennonite wife way, come out of the chicken coop with a basket of eggs and give Heaven and her cloud of dust a stare.

Heaven jumped out of the van. For ten miles, she had been going over the evidence against Ernest in her mind. He had been around for all the major events. He could loosely be construed a bread fanatic. He was religious, and his religion was historically connected to 'Red Turkey' wheat. So far, so good. Religious folks down through the ages had proven to have some pretty bloody ideas that they were sure came from God.

"I need to speak to Ernest," she demanded without any explanation. She could always apologize for her rudeness later if it turned out she was wrong. She was pretty sure she wasn't.

"Aren't you Del's sister," the wife asked, putting down the egg basket and holding out her hand.

Very nice, Heaven thought as she walked toward that outstretched hand and shook it. She put me in my place for rushing in here without any manners. "Yes, we met last week at the bread lunch. Do you know where Ernest is?"

"Why he took a truckload of wheat over to the big co-op, by Alma. He hasn't been gone more than fifteen minutes. Would you like a . . ."

Heaven hopped back in the van. "Thanks. I'll just go by there on my way home." She quickly backed out of the Powell's yard, leaving the wife watching her drive away with her hand up shading her eyes.

The sixteen miles to Alma were pure torture. Just as she had been so sure about Walter's guilt, now she was positive Ernest was the ergot killer.

The grain elevators at Alma were not like the little silo that stood behind the research lab in Manhattan where the general died. They were massive, at least forty silo stacks marking the skyline of Kansas. The silos were much taller as well, reaching almost a hundred feet in the air. Their profile was visible many miles away. Heaven gulped as she drew near. Although she had grown up practically in the shadow of these towering storage elevators, they had never seemed ominous before this week. Now she imagined the general flying off the top of this big puppy.

Just as Heaven was entering the ramshackle addendum

marked with the sign ELEVATOR OFFICE, two older men dressed in faded overalls came out. "Have you seen Ernest Powell," Heaven asked, blocking the way to their pickups with arms outstretched.

The two men didn't even hesitate. They ambled around Heaven with a chuckle and a gesture upward. "He's up there, putting his last batch of wheat in storage."

"Wait! Thanks. Two questions. How do I get up there? And wasn't the harvest over months ago?"

The two stopped at the front of their truck. "Right over there," the talkative one said, pointing to a door attached to the main body of the elevators. "The elevator is to the right there. And you're right about the harvest. Aren't you the O'Malley girl?"

Heaven blushed to be found out as a Kansas girl asking a dumb question about the wheat harvest. "Yes. Del's my brother."

"Well, little lady, the harvests have been so big the last two years that the elevators haven't had room for all the grain. There's wheat sitting on the ground all over the state. Enough moved out this month, Ernest got room for the last of his. Us too. Be careful up there now." The two grizzled men got in their truck and pulled away. It never occurred to them that they shouldn't leave the O'Malley girl alone with Ernest Powell, or vice versa for that matter.

Heaven stepped into the room built around the base of the silos. On one wall was a big chalkboard with various colors of chalk, pink for hard winter wheat, blue for soybeans, white for soft spring wheat, and so on. Forty round rings were drawn on the board and in each ring, writing in the appropriate color chalk indicated what was stored inside. Heaven stopped to see if they happened to put the name of the co-op member who had stored the grain in each tank, but no such luck. There were signs everywhere stating "GRAIN DUST IS LIKE EXPLOSIVES. NO SMOKING" and boxes of poison sitting stacked around. Heaven picked one up. "Weevil-cide" it said. Hydrogen phosphide. She dropped it quickly. It didn't sound good.

She walked over to the elevator, her footsteps ringing hollow in the high empty interior. She pressed the button and an ancient creak started a pulley up at the top of the building. The elevator was one technological step above the general's outside lift. It resembled the open ironwork elevators in Art Nouveau apartment buildings except, instead of scrolling ironwork, this elevator was a rusted metal cage. Heaven stepped in and pressed the top button. Except for the elevator mechanism, it was quiet. Heaven looked up. It was a long way up there. Why hadn't she asked the farmers to come up with her or at least stay around? Why hadn't she asked Ernest to come down to ground zero? She remembered no one knew where she was.

The elevator stopped with a jolt. Heaven swung the door open and stepped out, into a big, long room that ran across the top of all the silos. Every so often in the floor, there was an oversized manhole cover with the words DO NOT STEP stenciled on the top of them. Heaven assumed they were the covers to the silos themselves. She walked gingerly around each one.

In the middle of the room a door stood open. A "balcony" ran across the outside of the building. Heaven had looked up there when she arrived. It had seemed so high up in the air. Now she peeked her head out the door.

Ernest Powell was standing there, as if he were on the Riviera or something, leaning against the metal railing, pulling a loaf of bread apart and throwing bread in the wind. He turned and smiled at Heaven. "There is an ancient ceremony called the Tashlich. It's the casting of bread upon the waters of a lake or a stream to symbolically cast off our sins. Here in the earthbound Midwest, it seems right to cast the bread to the wind instead."

"Casting off your sins, eh Ernest? Could you be doing this little ceremony with ergot bread?"

Ernest took a bite of what was left of the loaf in his hand, then he handed a chunk of it to Heaven. "Honey whole wheat, straight from the bread machine." Heaven pitched hers off into space immediately.

"Ernest, what in the hell is going on in your mind? I know you're the damned maniac that planted bad flour all over, around, and through this bread conference."

"Please Heaven. No profanity."

"Fuck you, Ernest. My daughter was part of the crowd of people that I nursed through the night and took to the hospital this morning. A man is paralyzed. Two men are dead, and I have a sneaking suspicion that your neighbor should be added to the list. That's profanity as far as I'm concerned."

"Heaven, have you ever heard of an Examen of Conscience?"

"No, but I guess I'm about to," Heaven sighed. This wasn't going like she had hoped. Where are all those criminals who crack the minute Matlock or Perry Mason put a little pressure on them? Those two never had enough evidence for a conviction either.

"St. Ignatius, not that I believe in saints but I do admire the Jesuits," Ernest confessed as if he had confessed a taste for pornography. "St. Ignatius prescribed a daily discernment of spirits, an ongoing self-examination called the Examen of Conscience. I do that every time I make bread. I think about the last twenty-four hours and thank God for all the good that has come into my life. I know that I am in God's presence because God is most manifest in our most fundamental food, bread."

"And so I suppose God told you to do it?" Heaven asked.

"As I make bread, as the divine spirit guides me, I think about how I can be a better father, a better neighbor, a better man. When I discovered this blessed seed that creates bread that brings God right into a person, I knew I had to share it with those who really cared."

Heaven was encouraged. Ernest could be talking about ergot.

"And when the smell of fresh-baked bread fills every house in America, then the gift of life will belong to everyone. That's what I'm offering, the gift of life, Heaven." Ernest was surveying his universe, the Kansas farmland, with the bemused look of George Burns playing God.

"I have a feeling the general, and Dieter, and your neighbor, what was his name—Ben Akers—I have a feeling they wouldn't call it the gift of life," Heaven said.

"They have been joined with God," Ernest said serenely. "I'm sure they are divinely happy, Heaven. It's what we live for, isn't it, to be rejoined with the Creator?" Then he turned and went toward the door. "Have you ever seen how these elevators physically store the grain, Heaven? It's fascinating."

"So, Ernest. All that talk about the gift of life. That has a real Jim Jones ring about it. Are you planning to give away ergot flour with every free bread machine? Wipe out the nation's poor?" Heaven followed Ernest, glad to get off the balcony.

Ernest didn't seem to be playing question and answer anymore. He had his own agenda and any information Heaven acquired would be from the bits and pieces of his bread manifesto. He picked up a brass pole that looked like a curtain rod and had been propping the door open. "This is called a probe. When you bring a load of grain to any storage facility, they stick this probe down into the load. Then when they weigh your grain, they get a moisture content from the top and the bottom of your train car or truck load." Ernest demonstrated that by sliding the top of the probe around. Slits up and down the length of the brass rod were exposed and grain ran out on the floor.

Ernest leaned down and picked some kernels up and handed them to Heaven. She thought they were wheat but they didn't look normal. Think, think, she told herself. They were sticky, like something was seeping from the kernels. They were the wrong color too, a dark purple that was almost black. She remembered. The description of ergot in the medical books had mentioned both the color and the "honey" that oozes from infected grain.

"The trick was to get it to grow on wheat," Ernest explained calmly. "Rye was easy, the grasses in the cow pasture were easy, but it took some time to get it to attack wheat." Ernest took Heaven's arm firmly and guided her to the wrong end of this vast enclosed platform, the end away from the elevator that could take her down to the ground again.

"By the way, Ernest, where is the fellow who checks the grain with that probe?" Heaven said with as much of a cheerful tone as she could muster.

"This is a co-op, and I'm a member. I told Gene he could take a long lunch break, I'd watch things while my grain loaded," Ernest said as they neared a huge conveyor belt. The belt must have been three feet across and was going incredibly fast, as huge stainless steel bearings propelled it from some lower floor.

"How fast does that thing go?" Heaven asked.

Ernest pushed Heaven roughly down a small flight of stairs, to another vast room in which rubber conveyer belts ran in every direction. "Fifty or sixty miles an hour. They direct the grain to the correct silo, then," Ernest took the brass probe and smacked Heaven with it across her middle, like an ancient swordsman. She staggered backward. "In goes the grain and down a hundred feet." He hit Heaven again and again, until she fell, landing on her back on the conveyor belt. As she felt herself being pulled up an incline, she grabbed for the end of the probe and held on for dear life, knowing that it was connected to Ernest.

Ernest was caught off balance by Heaven's last-ditch attempt and he, too, fell on the conveyor belt. The belt was climbing toward the top of the building again. Heaven looked for a place to jump off but couldn't see anything to grab hold of. The grain made the rubber surface of the belt as slippery as a greased slide on a school playground. She looked at the dancing kernels all around her and realized they were dark purple. She was riding on the ergot wheat. She grabbed for the whirring edge of the belt and cut her hand right away but held fast with one hand while holding on to the pole with the other. She felt blood seeping out of her palm and her whole hand throbbed.

First, she had to get rid of Ernest. She started pushing on him with the tip of the probe, jabbing with as much strength as she could muster. Ernest was lying twisted on the belt with one leg bent under his body. He was trying to use the probe and Heaven's weight above him to help pull himself around.

"Stop this thing," Heaven screamed. "Help. Somebody help." She was jerking the probe with all her might, and Ernest was holding on with all his might. His hat had fallen off and his long hair and beard were flying wildly. The conveyor belt was on a fairly straight stretch right now, but was flying along five feet off the floor. Below, several of those manhole covers were open, exposing the opening through which the grains were loaded into the silos. Heaven didn't want to chance jumping if it meant she could end up buried in a hundred feet of soybeans.

But jumping didn't seem so bad when Heaven saw what was coming up. The conveyor belt had almost reached the end of the line. She could see a steep drop ahead and hear the rushing sound of grain falling like a waterfall. She dropped her end of the probe and got ready to bail out. A broken bone was better than suffocation. The belt fed the grain directly into one of those round holes on the floor, so the trick was to ride it close to the floor but without going over the lip into the abyss.

Heaven jumped, rolling over on to the floor with a thud. Ernest wasn't so lucky. When Heaven had suddenly let go of the brass pole, Ernest had tumbled down the belt, out of control. Just as he straightened himself out again, he rolled over the side.

"Dear God, take my spirit . . . oh, thank you, thank you. Heaven, help me. You have to help me." Ernest pleaded from the dark hole in the floor. Heaven crawled on her hands and knees over to the opening. Her ankle was badly twisted and her hand was still bleeding, but other than that she thought everything was still in one piece.

A guy wire hung down into the black emptiness. Heaven supposed that occasionally someone—it was hard to imagine a worse job—had to go down in these things. Maybe they clipped a safety belt to the wire. Right now, Ernest Powell was dangling on the wire about ten feet down. Heaven estimated the top of the pile of grain was another twenty feet below him. Heaven grabbed the wire but with one hand almost useless, she didn't think she had a chance in hell of pulling him up.

"Someone help us," she screamed at the top of her lungs. Then she peered down at Ernest who was slipping inch by inch towards his tainted grain. "Ernest, you say God is present when you make bread. Well, then he's sure to be down there with you now. I wish I could just walk away and leave you, you son of a bitch, but . . ." She pulled on the wire with both hands as hard as she could. Her blood trickled down on the dusty floor. Ernest rose a foot or so.

"Ernest, help me save you. Pull yourself up the wire." Ernest put one hand in front of the other but quickly slipped back and lost all he had gained.

"Heaven, tell my wife I love her," Ernest cried.

"Don't give up. You can't give up. You have to live to tell people about your cockamamy scheme. No one will ever believe me. What were you going to do with this trainload of bad wheat anyway, make the whole country see God whether they want to or not?"

"They want to," Ernest said, with the old conviction back in his voice.

Heaven gave a fierce pull on the wire. Suddenly it went slack in her hand. She peered over the side just in time to see the shadow that was Ernest disappear in that dim grain grave.

"Poisonous grain, seventy feet deep. Who says there isn't justice in the universe," Heaven muttered as she lay on the floor, panting from fear and exhaustion.

Butterscotch Brownies

½ cup melted butter
2 ½ cups light brown sugar
2 eggs
1 tsp. vanilla
1 cup sifted all purpose flour
½ tsp. salt
1 cup chopped walnuts

Add the brown sugar to the melted butter in a heavy sauce pan and stir until bubbly. Remove from heat and cool to room temperature. Add to other ingredients and mix. Bake in a greased 9 x 11 pan, 35 minutes at 325 degrees.

Butterscotch Sauce

1 ⅓ cups sugar, white or dark brown
¾ cup dark corn syrup
3 T. butter
2 T. water
4 T. heavy cream

Combine all ingredients but the cream in a heavy sauce pan. Slowly bring to a boil, stirring occasionally. Boil 5 minutes. Remove from heat, cool, and stir in cream, beating until the sauce has a satiny finish.

To make butterscotch sundaes, place a blond brownie on the serving plate, top with vanilla ice cream or frozen yogurt, and drizzle with commercial hot fudge topping and the butterscotch sauce. This is great with banana ice cream, too.

Sixteen

"Mom, come on. Say yes."

Heaven was driving around the airport circle drive for the fourth time. They still had so much to talk about. "I suppose it wouldn't kill me. I'll come."

Iris grinned and jumped up and down in her seat. She still looked very frail to Heaven but she insisted she was fine. "You haven't been to visit for two years. Come in November, for your birthday. I know you can't get away for the holidays but you can come for your birthday."

Heaven sighed and pulled the van over to the curb. "Okay, okay. I'll come to England for my birthday. Honey, are you sure you feel like this long trip? I wish you'd stay a few more days."

Iris gave her mother a stern look. "You wish I'd stay a few more years you mean. Can't you just see us, down on 5th Street in fifty years, with twin electric wheelchairs and you telling me I'm too young to leave home."

"I can't tell you how sorry I am that you were put in danger."

"Mom, I've done worse stuff on purpose."

"I don't want to know," Heaven said, smiling in spite of herself.

Iris opened the door and started piling her bags on the sidewalk. Heaven turned off the engine and went around the van to help. Iris gave her a sweet hug. "I'm sorry you almost ended up buried in grain. I thought Uncle Del was going to have to be taken off to the hospital when he got the call to come get you. He was hysterical when he called us."

"I'm just glad, well not really glad, but I'm just glad the bad grain was right there where Ernest fell. Those folks would never have believed that nice Ernest Powell was trying to feed the whole country LSD in their bread so they could be close to God. I'm sure most of them still think it was just a tragic mistake, that his mind was poisoned and he didn't know what he was doing."

Iris shook her head. "Well, it was and he didn't. Thank God that grain didn't get to the mill. It would have really caused a mess."

"As you know," Heaven said, her eyes filling up with tears.

Iris punched her Mom in the arm. "I know it would do no good to say don't cry and feel sorry for yourself but please try to enjoy it at least."

"I have until five this evening to feel miserable. Then I've got to pay attention. We have lots of reservations. There's some conference in town."

"It better not have anything to do with food," Iris said as she hugged her mother one last time.

"Dairy farmers, I'm afraid." Heaven said, and they both laughed.

"No mad cows, Mom. I'll see you in November." Iris turned to go inside the airport.

"Honey," Heaven said urgently.

Iris turned with a little smile. She wondered how many times it would take for her to finally get in the door. "Yes, Mom?"

"Say hello to Stuart for me, even though I still think he's too old and too rich for you."

Iris beamed. "I'll give him your love."

Heaven played listlessly with her latte. She was moping. She had cried all the way back from the airport, but she still wanted a little more time to feel pitiful.

Hank was gone for the weekend too, off to Chicago to some doctors' meeting. She couldn't bear the thought of going to the cafe, so she had come to the Classic Cup in Westport instead. The owner, Charlene Welling, came over to her table with a scone fresh out of the oven. "This'll make you feel better," Charlene prescribed.

Heaven pulled the snapshot from the accident in Manhattan, Kansas, out of her pocket. She had found it under one of Iris's open suitcases. Heaven peered at the guys in the hazmet gear. Was one of them Ernest? She honestly didn't know. Would it have prevented anything if she had found this photo sooner?

"Penny for your thoughts." It was Patrick Sullivan, the BIG BREAD research man. Only today, Patrick was in chef whites.

"Patrick, what are you doing here dressed like that?"

"Making your scone. Go ahead, taste it," Patrick said proudly. He sat down at Heaven's table.

Heaven took a bite. It was delicious. "Very buttery. How do you feel? But just because I asked how you feel don't think I've forgotten or forgiven you for the rats. What are you doing here?"

"Well, I saw God when I was tripping and he told me not to work for those clowns another day, that my soul was in danger. I went right over there on Thursday and told them I had an "experience," that I wouldn't be any good to them. Then I came over here and talked to Charlene. I'm the new baker and pastry chef. Please don't tell her what I did to you."

"Because she would fire your ass?" Heaven said with an malicious smile on her face.

"I made a terrible mistake. I will spend the next two years of my life trying to make it up to you. How about dinner tonight?"

Heaven shook her head. "You know better. I own a restaurant. I can't go out to dinner, and if I could go out to dinner, I certainly wouldn't go with you, someone who terrorized me in my own van."

"Breakfast, then, on Sunday? I know the restaurant is closed on Sunday."

"Maybe in a few months after you've been punished, maybe breakfast," Heaven said. "Now, you have to answer one question for me."

"Ask anything."

"Your company . . . "

"My ex-company remember," Patrick interjected.

"Your ex-company applied for a patent for something that they didn't really invent. My research says only the inventor can patent something, and he's dead. What do you think will happen to the perennial wheat clone?" Heaven asked.

"The BIG BREAD lawyers will argue that even though the research lab was an independent entity, at the time of the discovery, they were working for BIG BREAD, so any invention is the property of the BIG BREAD, or at least that's what I would argue," Patrick said.

"Boy, I'm glad you aren't on their side anymore. You have a sneaky mind."

Patrick pushed his glasses up on his nose. "I'll accept that as a compliment and wait to hear what my next sentence is. In the meantime, will you taste my new butterscotch brownie hot caramel sundae?"

Heaven smiled. "Bring it on, babe. There's nothing I like better than two rich baked goods products before eleven in the morning. It sets you up for the day."

Patrick picked up the photo. "What's this?"

"Old news, Patrick."

Patrick got up and held his hand out to Heaven. She shook it. "By the way," he said, "some time when it all isn't so fresh I'd like to hear what happened out there with Ernest and all. Now, I'm going to make you a sundae you won't forget."

"Deal," she said and slipped back into her funk. Heaven was glad for Patrick. Too bad she felt so sorry for herself.

"There you are. Thank God." It was Murray Steinblatz, looking frantic and happy at the same time.

"How'd you find me?" Heaven asked. "And what's wrong?"

"I knew you'd be depressed after you took Iris to the airport, so I figured you'd come here. You don't like to be around your staff when you're depressed."

"Everybody thinks they've done something wrong when I'm depressed. Today, nobody did anything except Iris. She left. It's just that old I-hate-to-let-go syndrome. I'll be fine tomorrow. Answer my second question. What's the matter?"

A server brought the butterscotch brownie extravaganza and she and Murray both dug in with due diligence for a minute.

"Nothing's the matter. I wrote it."

"Wrote what, Murray? Oh, your first new piece for the *Times?*"

Murray beamed and pulled some sheets of paper out of his old corduroy sports coat. "It's all about the bread conference."

Heaven looked doubtful. "I don't know Murray. I don't think they're ready for that story in New York."

Murray took another bite of ice cream and brownie. "No," he mumbled with his mouth full. "No," this time with his mouth empty, "I didn't tell them the whole story. I'm saving that for a screenplay. It'll make a terrific made for television movie, H. No, I just told them all about Walter and the perennial polycultures and how we have all our eggs in one basket when it come to grains and God knows what else. I went out and talked to Walter yesterday and then stayed up almost all night writing."

"How was Walter?"

"Better. Boy did he have some good pot. We got stoned and had a ball talking."

"I don't want to know the gory details, please. So, have you sent the column off yet?"

"Yep," Murray said, with that look on his face that was a mixture of panic and joy. "Faxed it about nine."

"And?" Heaven could tell there was an "and", she just couldn't make out if it was good or bad.

"And they loved it. Said it was great stuff. Thought they

should do a piece on the science page about GRIP or maybe it was on the business page. Anyway, babe, I'm a hit!"

"Again, Murray." Heaven reminded him. "You're a hit, again."

Heaven, perked up by Murray's good news, took another bite of ice cream.

Recipe Index